IN

As a pirate, I tend to hang out with unsavory outcasts at the edges of the known universe. I'm used to running into thieves, assassins and fugitives. It shouldn't surprise me to see a forbidden human female for sale in the tunnels of the space station, but I hate it. When I see she's near death, I have to act.

I buy her.

She spits in my face.

It's love at first sight.

At least, it's love at first sight on my end. I know it can never be, though, because I'm an ugly beast of an alien to her. The enemy. If only she knew just how many laws I'd be willing to break for one taste of her lips...

IN THE CORSAIR'S BED

RUBY DIXON

Photo by: Sara Eirew Photographer

Cover by: Kati Wilde

Edits by: Aquila Editing

❀ Created with Vellum

1

TAREKH

*T*he busy hum of the cantina almost—*almost*—drowns out Alyvos's sulking.

Almost.

My drinking partner stares at his refreshment bubble dispenser with a sour look on his hard face. "I still don't see why they need to take time away."

Again with this? I'm an easy-going male but Alyvos's fixation with the captain and his new mate is beginning to get on my nerves. "It's like I said before, they're newly mated. They want time alone together. It's a human tradition."

"Yes, well, the captain is mesakkah, and we all know that humans are…" he pauses, as if realizing his audience isn't receptive.

I know what he wants to say. Humans are crude. Humans are half civilized. Humans are strange. I don't know that he's wrong, but I also don't think he's completely correct, either. From what I know of Fran, she seems clever, and she's just as civilized as any mesakkah female in her way. Humans are strange, though. I can't deny that. I just shrug and pluck one of his refreshment bubbles out of the air since he seems to be ignoring them. I pop it into my mouth and lick my fingers. "They're happy. Leave them be."

"We should be pushing for another job," Alyvos says, sliding his bubble dispenser out of my reach. "Squeeze a few more credits in."

I just snort at that. If there's anyone who cares less about money in the crew of the *Dancing Fool*, it's Alyvos. He's ex-military and doesn't see fit to spend his credits unless it's an emergency. It's not that he's cheap, he just lives a very austere life and doesn't see the point of good food, drinks, gambling, or females. You know, any of the fun stuff. Kef, even the refreshment bubbler he's hiding from me I purchased for him because he seemed in a foul mood tonight. "Because you need more credits?" I tease him and then nod at the dancer on the stage. "Gonna shell out a few and try to get that one in your bed tonight?"

Alyvos just glares at me and cracks his knuckles. He really is bringing the mood in this corner of the cantina down. Haal Ui is a mess of a space station on most days. It's full of pirates and degenerates, thieves, whores and anything else that likes the shadowy fringes of society. Probably why it's one of our favorite hangouts. It's a mess, but in that mess, you can have a lot of fun.

Here, no one seems to notice that Captain Sav Kivian Bakhtavis has a female human with him. Human slaves might be illegal in the Allied Federation of Worlds, but they're pretty common in the dregs of society here. Reedy music begins to play and I glance up at the stage. A lithari female is gyrating up there while interested males watch her jiggle and bounce. They're a little too placid-looking for my tastes, but the bouncing is rather attractive. I tear my gaze away from the fluid slide of her four teats and press a button to request a refill for my refreshment bubbler. "You kinda seem like you're itching for a fight," I point out. "And Bakhtavis ain't here to fight."

Alyvos shrugs, glaring at his bubbler.

"And it'd probably make Fran cry, and I know you don't like that." For all his sharp words, Alyvos likes the female. She's a tough little thing. Kef, we all like her. Even Sentorr, who wouldn't know how to relax if relaxing bit him on the tail.

Alyvos just shakes his head. "It's just not military to have slaves on board."

Ah. Alyvos gets touchy whenever something reminds him just how far he's fallen from his military days. There are a lot of sore feelings there, and those usually explode out in a fistfight, and then Aly goes back to his normal surly self. Maybe that's what all this griping's about. He's trying to pick a fight with me.

Gonna be a long haul on that one, because I ain't the type to pick a fight with my friends. I'll have his back in a heartbeat, but I'm not gonna start slugging on him because he's cranky. 'Sides, I'd probably mess up his pretty face with my fists. Aly's in good shape, but I'm a monster. No one ever believes I'm just the medic on the *Dancing Fool*. They think I'm the muscle. Me and Aly both fill that role, though. Alyvos is a whiz with weapons. I'm just brute force. Together, we get shit done, though.

Alyvos watches as a bubble rises from his refreshment station and then pops it, spilling his drink all over the table. "I don't like it. Just feels wrong."

"Good thing you're not the captain, then. You don't have to like it. You just have to live with it," I tell him easily. "And gimme your bubbler if you're not going to drink, because that's a waste of perfectly good brew. If you're gonna be like this, you can go sit back in the ship with Sentorr."

He turns narrowed eyes on me, even as the music changes and a few more females join the lithari on stage. Alyvos hasn't even peeked in their direction. He really is cranky. "How can you be so content with it? She's going to get a share. She's going to breathe our oxygen. Ship costs are going to go up. All so the captain can get his cock wet? How does that make you happy?"

I shrug. "'Cause Bakhtavis is happy, and he's a friend. And I like Fran. Or are you mad because she ate all your chski pickles?"

"She did?"

Whoops. "Maybe. Maybe not. I'm sure we can get some more on the station here. Can get a lot of stuff, if you're in the mood, and you're not ugly like me." I grin at a nearby female who's wandering close to our table, probably drawn by Alyvos's too-pretty features. She flinches backward at the sight of me, turning in the other direction. Yep. Typical female. I can get my cock wet if I need to, but I hate payin' for a female to grit her teeth through a mating.

I'd rather just drink.

The music gets louder, and people start rising from their chairs to see what the females are doing on stage. The crowd suddenly seems a bit more chaotic, and my trained senses are immediately alert. "I just don't see—" Alyvos begins, and then someone shoves his chair, knocking his hand into his bubbler and splashing the next serving all over the arm of his tunic.

Ah, kef. Here we go.

Alyvos's eyes light up. He senses the fight he's been wanting, and he jumps to his feet, fists at the ready, tail flicking. The kaskri that shoved his chair gives him a scathing look and then dashes off.

Uh oh. Something tells me that wasn't just an accident.

Aly comes to the same conclusion. He pats his pocket and then snarls. "He got my credit chits."

Pickpocket. Now it's not just Alyvos looking for a fight anymore. I get to my feet and tap the button to cash us out. "Go after him. I'll follow."

He cracks his knuckles again, eyes ablaze with bloodthirsty enthusiasm. Alyvos winds through the crowd with single-minded determination, and even though a tall, horned mesakkah is easy to make out in this crowd, he disappears as I wait for the processor to cash out my table. I hate missing a fight, but I also don't shit where I eat, and we do a lot of business at the Haal Ui cantina. I make sure we stay on the up and up with the owners, because they'll look the other way at a lot of stuff, but not at stiffing 'em on the bill.

The old, cranky machine chimes that I've paid, and then I grab one last refreshment bubble and swipe a hand over my mouth. Hope that idiot doesn't start a fight without me. That's no fun. I move my way out of the cantina, snarling at people when the crowd doesn't part quickly enough. Then I'm free of the oppressive crowd, and the recycled air in the hallway feels like a keffing cool breeze after the humidity of the cantina. I glance around, but I don't see Alyvos, just the usual lurkers in the dark halls of Haal Ui station. Couple of females loiter in shadowy doorways, looking to make extra credits. Two male sszt stand together, talking in low voices and eyeing the women. Farther down the hall, I can see a crowd watching something. Probably gambling, or fenced goods. Alyvos won't be there. I slide a hand up my arm, activating my wristband, and then search for Alyvos's bio-signal with my tracker. Farther down the hall. Looks like he's heading toward the docks, and at a fairly fast pace. Chase must still be on.

I head down the hall, my steps slow and steady. The whores glance over at me and I nod at them in greetin', because I'm a nice keffing guy. "Ladies."

One looks appalled. The other lifts her chin. "Want a good time, friend? Tightest cunt in three systems, right here." She grabs between her thighs.

"'Preciate the offer, but I'm hunting down a friend. Maybe next time."

She winks at me as if we're friends, but her expression shows a flicker of relief. Can't say I blame her. I'm big, even for a mesakkah, and I'm not handsome. Her gaze is all business as she sizes up the next male to come out of the bar and I keep on going. I'll let Aly get in a few punches before I try to break things up.

I pass by the gamblers, clustered at one bend in the hallway, and keep on going. It's almost as crowded out here in the snaking halls as it was in the cantina. Damn. I make a mental note to tell Kivian that the next time he wants privacy with Fran, maybe he picks a less busy time to hang out at the station. Two more bends later, I'm still not caught up with Alyvos and his thief, but I'm running into even more people. There's another cluster of people, this one all males, and my hackles go up a bit. As I walk past, there's a lot of low laughter and the men immediately move closer together as if they want to block my view. Someone gives me an ugly look when I walk a bit too close. Well now, that's cute. They must be shoppin' something that they don't want competition on. Just to piss 'em off, I pause and pretend to look over the goods.

Females. Probably slaves. I let my gaze wander over them as if I'm interested. Truth be told, I find it a pretty appalling way to make a living, taking other people's rights away. Just because it's legal on a lot of worlds doesn't mean I have to agree with it. I let my gaze roam over the females as one is trotted forward in a neck collar and wrist-chains and nothing else. She shakes her teats at me and I'm reminded of the dancer back in the club.

"Slaves for sale," the ooli male holding a datapad and leaning against the wall tells the group. He sounds bored, scratching at his gut before eyeing the crowd. "Good prices. All kinds."

The naked female takes this as her cue. "Want to buy me?" she asks, so forward and unafraid. "I'll never be able to tell you no."

My gut twists. I may be ugly, but I have standards. I smile at her, hiding my feelings. "'Fraid your price is outside of my credit limit, pretty one."

She smiles and turns around, shaking her bottom and showing her stubby tail off to buyers. The male next to me—another szzt —looks interested, and she saunters up to him, putting her arm around his neck.

I push through the crowd of men, done here.

Then, I pause.

And take a few steps backward.

As the female slave gyrates and teases the buyers, I notice for the first time that not all of the slaves look so enthusiastic to be bought. There are a few sitting along the wall, all the spirit gone from them. They're nothing out of the ordinary when it comes to slaves, sadly enough, and I make a mental note to tell Kivian about this in case we can do something. Off in one corner, though, at the end of the line of slaves, there's a huddled heap.

There's a flash of pinkish-golden flesh that reminds me of Fran, though. And that's what makes me stop. Because if this guy has humans...I don't know if I can walk past. Not since I know Fran like I do. I know that she's a kind, funny, compassionate being, and I can't help but see her in the shadows. I head over to the end of the line and kneel down.

There's a heap of delicate limbs, a little paler than Fran's. But the structure is the same, and the facial features. Maybe I don't know enough about humans, but they look alike to me. This one's got a dirty brown mane instead of Fran's dark one, but other than that, they could be sisters. This one is covered in bruises and half of her face is swollen. There's a gash across one cheek that is crusted over and possibly infected. She doesn't get up when I come over, her breathing shallow. Lacerations and bruises cover a lot of her naked body, to the point that I'm surprised I could tell by the coloration that she's human at all.

"Hello," I say in the Earth tongue.

No response. Perhaps she's barely conscious. Either way, I can't walk past and leave. I glance over at the bored slaver. "What's the story behind this one?"

He shrugs, typing something into his datapad. "Human. Sick one, though. They're not very hardy creatures. Still got a tight cunt, though. You want a round?"

"How much to buy her? Take her home with me?"

The seller frowns. "You want to buy her? Friend, she doesn't have much juice left in her. It's a bad bargain on your half, and humans are expensive."

I shrug. "Humor me."

He names a price that's more than I'll make even with a year of pirating. Luckily, I have access to the credit account of the *Dancing Fool* in case of emergencies, and I haggle with him. She's sick, after all. No one's going to buy her in this condition. I might be the only interested buyer he gets. Surely he can come down on the price a bit more for an interested buyer.

We go back and forth. I try not to look over at the female because that might convey my interest more than just as a curious bargain-hunter. Every instinct in me as a medic says that she needs immediate attention, though. Her wounds look infected, and as fragile as humans are, I'm not entirely convinced she doesn't have a rib through a lung. Just the thought of someone keffing her while she's this injured makes my brain boil with anger. By the time we agree to a price that would make Kivian reach for his blaster if he knew what I was spending, I'm ready to crack my knuckles like Alyvos and knock some heads together. It takes everything I have to calmly hand him my credit chip and wait for him to scan it. Then, the amount's transferred into his account, he nods, and I'm given the electronic key to her cuffs and collar. "All yours, friend." He's doing his best not to smirk, clearly thinking I've made a fool's bargain.

Maybe I have. But the medic in me can't let this go.

I move to the end of the line and touch the human's shoulder. "You're coming with me."

She looks up, her eyes glassy, and it takes a moment for them to focus on me. I notice her pupils are dilated. She must be in a lot of pain. Her mouth pulls back at the corners and I'm fascinated at the thought of her smiling at me—

But then she spits in my face.

The crowd laughs. I don't care. I wipe the spit off my face and oddly enough, I'm smiling. If she's got that much anger in her, she's a fighter. "Can you stand?"

Her eyes narrow at me and she doesn't respond.

All right, then. "I'm going to pick you up." I slide my arms under her carefully and do my best to not harm her, but she feels more fragile and broken the moment I lift her. I can hear her suck in a breath and then she goes completely limp, passed out from the pain.

I'm going to beat every keffing asshole that touched her. "Why's she so messed up?" I ask the seller as I carefully cradle her in my arms. "You do know your merchandise will last longer if you take care of it."

The seller just snorts, not looking up from his datapad. "She's not the friendliest type. But there's people that pay for that kind of thing, and pay well."

All right. I'm going to take her back to the *Fool*, and then I'm going to come back here and choke the keffing daylights out of this one. "Gotcha."

I leave. I have to, or I'm going to murder him right here and right now, and I've got too much on my plate at the moment. I have to check on Alyvos to make sure he doesn't need backup, and I have to fix my human. As priorities go, he's lower on the scale. I make a mental note to come back later, and then I head down the hall, tracking Alyvos by his locator.

I run into him in the halls, leaving one of the docking bays. His knuckles are bloody and his lip is split, but he grins with smug satisfaction as he meets my eyes. "Looks like I'm too late for the fight."

"It wasn't much of a fight," he says, and cracks those keffed-up knuckles anyhow. A moment later, he realizes I'm holding something—someone—and pauses. "What is that?"

"A human."

His eyes go wide. "You bought a human? Why?"

"Because I couldn't leave her." It's clear to me that she needed my help. I wouldn't leave a friend behind, and I'm not leaving this fragile one to her fate. "If you're done here, I'm heading back to the ship. She needs patching up."

Alyvos grunts, but the restless fire is gone from his eyes. Whatever it was that was eating at him earlier, it's been calmed by a good bruising round of fighting. "Do I want to know how much she cost?"

"No. You really don't." But I would have paid it no matter what. I don't guess he needs to know that, either. I just cradle my burden in my arms and head for the dock housing the *Dancing Fool*.

Alyvos is gonna find out how much she cost when Kiv gets back anyhow and sees how much of the ship's money I've spent.

2

TAREKH

"He's got a what?" Sentorr's shout echoes through the *Fool's* bridge as Alyvos and I enter the ship.

I ignore it. Sentorr can be cranky at me later. Right now, I need to get my little female medical attention. She's still slumped against my shoulder, and her weight is so slight that I worry she's breaths away from slipping into death. The thought fills me with helpless rage as I think of her bruises and the casual way her last "owner" spoke.

I don't tend toward rages—that's Alyvos's speciality—but right now I'm torn between taking care of her and racing back into the tunnels to choke the life out of the man I bought her from.

But then she moans in pain, and I forget everything but her. She needs me. I head toward the med-bay of the ship and the doors open automatically at my bio-signature. I duck to enter the threshold and kick aside a roll of gauze bandages that has fallen from a shelf onto the floor. The place is a mess, but I work well in chaos. I shove the piled gadgets off of the examination table and gently lay her down. She's dwarfed in a mesakkah-sized bed, and for a moment, I worry that all of my equipment is going to be too large to help her.

"What is going on?" Sentorr demands, and I can hear his heavy boots stomping down the hall. Alyvos mumbles something, probably right behind him. I move to the door of the med-bay and shut it in their faces, because I need to concentrate on my patient.

I return to the female's side and get out my knife, cutting the filthy rags she's wearing off of her body. They don't cover much, and all they seem to be doing is sticking to her wounds. I need to see what's damaged and how badly she's hurt. "Computer, full body scan and diagnostic, please," I say as I slice away at her clothing.

Her eyes flutter open and she makes a low groan in her throat that sounds as ragged as she looks.

"It's all right," I tell her, switching to the human tongue. I added it to my language chip when Fran arrived, and while the words are unusual and harsh-sounding, they come easily enough. "You're safe now."

The female's head tilts slightly and then she looks right at me. I wait for her to suck in a breath. To comment on how ugly I am. I wasn't born cute, and after a shuttlebus accident as a youth destroyed what little charm I had, I figured it wouldn't matter if my nose got broken in every fight. It has...and my brow ridges and my cheek. I know I'm a mess. I grin at her to do my best to look friendly despite my ugly mug.

She just closes her eyes again, her body limp. I wonder if she even saw me.

Doesn't matter. She'll get a good look soon enough.

3

CATRIN

My newest customer is a demon.

Either he's a new customer, or I'm dead. Dead would work.

Of course, everything wouldn't hurt so badly if I was dead. That must mean I'm still alive. That must mean I'm this guy's whore for a night or however long he's bought me. The lights in this room are bright, which tells me I'm out of Haal Ui station. And he spoke English to me, which tells me that I'm not his first human "companion." Okay, so I'm dealing with a fetishist. It won't make me feel guilty to hurt him, then, because fuck him for buying a human to stick his dick into.

I pretend to be unconscious for a little longer, just to see how the demon reacts. He's busy cutting my clothes away from me, but I don't care about those. They're nasty and caked with blood and refuse anyhow. Clothing his slaves isn't a high priority for Yekkl, since we'll be taking them off again anyhow. I bite back a yelp of pain when one bit of fabric sticks to a fresh wound and agony sears up my side, but my new customer notices it anyhow.

"Sorry about that. Gotta get all of this garbage out of that wound before I seal it up."

Seal it up? Interesting. Maybe he's got a cleanliness fetish, too. Wouldn't be the worst I've had, considering. I'd love to be clean. And since he knows I'm awake, I open my eyes a crack and watch him through my lashes.

The demon-alien is fearsome looking. I've seen all kinds of mind-boggling aliens in the last few months, ever since I've been captured. This one is more humanoid than some, but in a dark, dangerous sort of way. His skin is a deep blue, his eyes pupilless and pale yellow. Massive horns arch back over his head like an antelope and are covered in shiny metal. When he smiles at me, he's got fangs. His face is a little messed up with scars and his features look like they don't completely line up, like something was repaired once and badly.

One arm moves over me and I see tattoos covering his skin. He's wearing a sleeveless top of some kind and it makes me realize just how muscled those bare arms are, and how big he is compared to me. Hell, his lower arm is probably as big around as my thigh. This guy's built like nothing I've ever seen before, and that's the scariest part. Some of the aliens I've run into, I thought I stood a chance because we were of a similar height or weight. I'd fight, hoping that desperation would make up for malnourishment and abuse, but it never did.

I shouldn't fight this guy, though. He'll snap me like a twig.

Doesn't mean I won't, of course. Fighting's what I do. I'll never stop fighting, because if I do, then I'm dead—both inside and out.

So as he runs a scanner-type object over my body, I carefully look around for something to use as a weapon.

This place is a mess, I have to say. There's junk piled on every available counter-space, and some of it looks like it's covered in motor oil. He pushes aside a tool of some kind as he pulls something else out of a box, and I see a giant needle filled with a bright liquid. Oh, fuck me. I hate needles.

I must make a sound of fear, because his gaze immediately flicks back to me. "This is going to hurt," he cautions. "It's going to sting and burn at the injection site, but then you'll feel a bit better. It's a cocktail of stimulants and vitamins because I'm showing you're deficient in several areas, and it should help your sluggish *kthf-sions*. I don't know the word in your language, sorry." He gives me a crooked grin. "Let's just say it's important. You need your strength."

I want to ask just what I need my strength for, but I learned a while back to stop asking, because I'd never like the answers. No one ever wants a slave strong for anything good. They only want a slave that can endure. I remain quiet and close my eyes when the needle gets closer. It presses against my bad side—where the asshole kicked me three days ago until I passed out—and I can feel my body break out in a cold sweat. Fuck, that hurts. Fuck, I hate needles.

"I know," the demon murmurs, and his voice sounds sympathetic. "I'm sorry."

I don't buy it. If I believed everything one of my captors told me... I open my eyes when the burning stops, because he's right. There's something pouring through my veins that feels a little tingly and cold, but in a good way. Refreshing, even.

Well, if he was dumb enough to shoot me with something that gives a burst of energy, I'm going to take it and use it. I watch as he sets the gigantic (now empty) needle down on the table and then digs through another box for something else. "I've got something over here that'll bind that wound of yours on your cheek without leaving much of a scar. Just gotta find it."

He turns his back to me and I quickly grab the needle gun and slide it under my arm, hiding it with my hand. It's not a very big weapon compared to this guy, but if I jab it into the right spot, I think I can kill him. Aren't people always dying in movies when they get stabbed in the neck with a needle? I clench it in my hand. Worth a shot.

When he turns around and leans over me again, I decide that it's time. I clasp the needle-gun in my hand and stab it into his neck with all the force I have in my body.

Or at least, I try to.

He's bigger than I anticipate despite things, and so I don't quite reach his neck, just his shoulder. And it doesn't actually sink in. It just bounces off of him with a bone-jarring thud that makes me wonder if he's wearing armor underneath that space-age muscle-shirt.

At any rate, I fail. The needle goes flying across the cluttered floor and my arm reverberates with pain, so much so that I feel as if I'm going to black out again. "Fuck."

The man stares at me, not moving. For a long moment, I think he's going to murder me. Just reach across the bed and choke the life out of me.

Instead, he smiles again. "Did you just try to kill me? Kef, that's cute."

"Fuck you," I tell him, frightened. I'm sure he's going to retaliate. He's just waiting for me to drop my guard. I try to push backward on the bed, to put space between us, but my body isn't responding. My arm feels like it snapped just from the reverberations of trying to stab him, and I've got nothing left in the tank. If I have to get off this table and run away, it'll be more of a crawl.

But I'll do it if I have to.

His mouth purses and he tilts his head. "Fuck is a human word for mating? I think my language chip must be malfunctioning." He puts a big finger into his ear and wiggles it as if he heard wrong.

"It's an insult," I spit at him. When he reaches for me with a gunlike blinking device, I shy backwards, raising my hands. "Don't fucking touch me!"

"Ah. Fuck is like kef. Handy insult, that. If you really want to fight back at a mesakkah with words, use 'kef.' I promise you'll get a better response." He reaches out and grabs my flailing wrists in a humiliatingly easy move, and then I'm pinned down to the table. "Stop moving or you're going to get gel all over the table."

"Gel so you can stick your monster cock inside me?" I thrash against his grip, but it's useless.

He grins. I think it's supposed to be terrifying, but it just pisses me off. "Gel so your wounds can heal their infections. I swear you've got dirt ground into them. And thank you for the compliment. I've had no complaints about my cock in the past, but it's nice to hear it reaffirmed. Face yes, cock no."

I scowl at him and jerk my arms again.

"Stop doing that or I'll have to use restraints. I'm serious." He holds up the medical-looking gun. "This shit's expensive and I'm already tapped out from buying you."

"Poor baby," I snarl at him, but I don't move. Once someone

mentions "restraints" it's all over. The last thing I want is to be chained up again, because then there's no chance of escape at all.

He leans over me and I have to bite back a wave of fear, because he's so massive. But all he does is pinch the swollen sides of my cheek together and runs a bead of gel down the wound. His brows look too hard for him to frown, but the tip of a blue tongue sticks out between his teeth as he works, as if he's trying very hard to be delicate. "There," he says after a moment. "We should keep your face nice and pretty."

I just scowl at him, because I'm not sure what else to do. He's being nice, but nice can also be a trap. Nice is the bait to let down my guard.

"Your ribs are cracked and you've got some bad internal bruising, but there's nothing that some painkillers won't fix and some rest. And this." He glances around and then snorts. "Well, okay, I was going to show you some synth-bandages, but I can't seem to find them."

"That's because you're a slob," I tell him. Now that he's released my hands, I can touch the sore spot on the left side of my body. He's not wrong, it feels swollen and hot when I skate my finger-tips over it, and I wince inwardly. It's been hurting for days to the point that I've been afraid to touch it, because I can't do anything about it.

"You're not wrong," he says cheerfully, and begins to poke through the clutter on one of the counters. "Aha," he says, and grabs a battery-sized blue bundle. "Here we go. Can you sit up?"

"Why?"

"So I can wrap this around your ribs." He shakes the small cylinder at me. "I mean, I can do it while you're lying down, but it'll be awkward for both of us that way."

I imagine him leaning in and pressing his big face against my boobs as he wraps my ribs—if that's actually what he's going to do—and mentally shudder. No, thank you. "I can sit up."

He waits as I struggle to sit upright. He doesn't offer an arm, which I appreciate, because I wouldn't take it anyhow. Getting myself into a seated position from lying down is rough. My body screams a painful protest and I suck in a breath from the pain, but I eventually manage to hunch somewhat upright. It's then that I remember that I'm naked. He cut all my clothes off of me, and I brace myself as he moves closer to my side.

"These bandages are waterproof and have numbing agents that are absorbed through the skin," he tells me as he begins to peel the "battery" apart. "After this, you can shower and we'll get you some fresh clothes. Sound good?"

Again, I wonder why he's being nice to me. I try to shrug, but it hurts too much.

"Leaning in now," the big ugly devil tells me, and I appreciate the warning in advance. His face moves close to mine as he puts his arms around my waist and then presses the edge of the bandage carefully against my skin. I bite back a whimper, and then there's a cooling numbness that feels so good that I relax a bit. He's all business as he winds the bandage around my ribs, and quiet. After a few loops around my torso, he finally speaks. "You're a fighter, aren't you? That how you got so torn up?"

"Maybe." I don't like giving information. It can be used against you.

"Good," he says, and I'm surprised. I look into his face, but he's not looking at me, just at the bandages. My breasts are already covered by the first two loops of them, so I know he's not ogling my tits. "You keep fighting all the time," he tells me. "Never let anyone think they own you or you'll start to think it, too."

Again, I don't understand why he's being so nice to me. Fear prickles up my spine, because I keep waiting for the trap. For the other shoe to drop. "What about you?" I can't help but ask.

He shrugs, those massive shoulders moving in a fluid, graceful sort of way. He finishes wrapping the bandages and then turns around to pick up something else and I realize he's got a tail. Wow, that's weird. It flicks back and forth, just like a cat's, the movements calm and easy. "I'm a fighter, but I don't have the heart for it like some. It's just a handy tool—"

"That wasn't what I meant," I interrupt.

The big alien turns and looks at me again, his eyes curious. He's less scary the longer I look at him, which is good. "What did you mean, then?"

"You said don't let anyone own me. What about you?"

"Oh. That." He scratches at his head. It's completely bald, the occasional pale scar marring the blue of his skin. "Yeah, I bought you, but not for keeps."

"How many nights, then?" It won't be so bad to be owned by this guy for a while, I guess. Beats having to do my nights in the tunnels. Those are the worst, when it feels like my soul is withering inside my body minute by minute by what I have to do.

He just scratches his head, like I've asked something weird that he doesn't know how to answer. "It's not like that," he says after a moment. "I bought you from him. You're not going back."

A knot forms in my throat. Surely he's not telling the truth? I've lived in that hell for so many months that I can't believe it's over, just like that. "You're lying," I manage.

"I'm not. I cleaned out the ship to buy you. Couldn't leave you there."

"So you're my new owner," I finally manage. I can live with that, I think. It doesn't matter if he's cruel or kind, as long as he's predictable. The worst is not knowing what to expect the next day.

His face darkens at the base of his horns, and he rubs his jaw with one big tattooed hand. "Actually, no. I didn't buy you because I need a bed slave. You belong to you."

4

———————

TAREKH

*S*he doesn't believe me. That's obvious.

It's all right. I'll give her time. It's understandable, given what I suspect she's been through. I'm impressed by the strength in her, from the fiery spark in her strange human eyes to her quiet stubbornness. Whatever they put her through, it didn't break her.

I like her spirit. It makes me glad I rescued her. Expensive, maybe, but the right thing to do.

She cleans off in the steamer, and I'm tempted to let her have time alone, but the equipment in the med-bay is expensive and she's already shown she's willing to snatch things and use them as weapons. I'm more concerned she'll hurt herself than me, so I lurk in the doorway of the water-closet until she emerges, wrapped in a towel, and gives me a defiant look. "Clothes?"

"Right this way." I give her a jaunty little salute, because I love that she's not afraid to demand things. I don't know what kind of shit life has handed her, but I like that she hasn't let it destroy her.

I open the doors to med-bay. Standing on the other side are both Sentorr and Alyvos, arms crossed and disapproving looks on their faces. They've clearly been waiting for me—for us—to emerge. I raise a hand in the air. "You both can yell at me in a minute, but for now, I'm getting our newest crewmember some clothes." I make sure to say the words in her human language so she can follow them.

Sentorr's jaw drops. Alyvos scowls. "Newest crewmember? Did you forget that this is a four-person runner?"

"It was. Then it was five when Fran came on board. Now it's six. See how that works? I'm good at math." I wink at him and then put my hands on his shoulders, firmly moving him aside so the little human has someplace to walk. "Now move. Come on." I pause and turn back to the human female. "I didn't get your name, did I?"

"I didn't offer it," she tells me in a tart voice, her chin up. I notice she's hugging the towel a little tighter to her, and her shoulders are tense at the sight of the rest of the crew.

"Well, until then, I'll call you...Roosha. That's a nice name." Old-fashioned, but pretty. I like it.

"That's shit," Alyvos says. "The kef kinda name is Roosha?"

"My mother's name was Roosha," Sentorr says, an odd expression on his face.

Kef me. It gets real quiet.

"Oh, whatever. Just call me Catrin," the human says. "Can we please get me some clothes now, or is this part of a grand plan to keep me naked?"

"No naked," Sentorr says, a fierce frown on his face. He points at me, all bottled frustration. "When you're done here, come to the mess. We need to talk about all this." He turns on his heel and storms back toward the bridge, and Alyvos follows him after sending me another surly look. I ignore their pouting. They'll get over it soon enough. I turn back to the female. "Cat-rn?"

"Cat, as in meow, and trin, as in 'rhymes with fin.'" I try again, and she shrugs. "Close enough. Your language is odd. All swallowed sounds."

"And yours is jarring," I tell her cheerfully. "All nasal honking and spitting. Come on, Catrhnnn, my room is this way."

"On second thought, just call me Cat. And why are we going to your room?" She pauses in the hall, uncertainty on her face. "I thought you said—"

"I did. We're not going for that." I can feel the base of my horns get hot at the suggestion. She looks so offended that it's downright embarrassing. I can see why she'd think that, though. Male like me has to buy his cunt, because I'm too ugly for most. "I don't have the passcode to get into the captain's chambers to borrow some of Fran's gear, so you're stuck wearing some of my castoffs. Hope that's all right. We can buy you some stuff out at the station, but it'll be a few hours before it gets here."

"Oh. Okay." Her skeptical glance moves over me. "I'm not sure anything you have will fit."

"I'm sure I have a tiny square of cloth somewhere." When she gives a little snort with amusement, I'm charmed. "So...Cat?"

"Yeah."

"My name is Das Tarekh Vesemmos, but everyone calls me Tarekh."

"I can't pronounce any of that," she protests.

"No translation chip?"

"No what?"

I grunt. "Never mind." That's something we can solve later. It just makes me angry that her captors—I won't call them owners—were too cheap to even give her a bulb translator. I guess no one cared if she could understand what they were saying. Pisses me off, though. Keffing thoughtless. I say my name again slowly so she can learn it, and this time she repeats it. "Tarekh." Her tongue seems to have trouble moving around the syllables, and it has a weird hiss when she says it.

I decide I like the hiss. "That's me." I lumber down the hall, assuming she's following me. The *Fool* isn't very big, and my chamber's one of the first ones in the personal quarters area of the ship. I flick my hand over the bio-meter and the doors slide open...and my boots flop out onto the hallway. I absently scoop them up and toss them back into the room. "Here we go."

"Jesus," the female breathes. Not "female," I correct myself. Cat. She stares at my chamber with a look of horror. "What is this, the alien version of *Hoarders*?"

Her words make no sense to me and I scratch at my shaved scalp as she gazes at my stuff from the safety of the hallway. My chambers do look a little messy. There's laundry on the floor and my uniform changes are tossed into a pile of clean-ish clothes so I know where to find 'em. I've been taking apart a few broken plasguns to try and improve them and the parts are scattered in another corner. And there might be a collection of vids in one corner that a nice female probably shouldn't see. "Wasn't expecting company," I tell her, kicking aside the junk in the doorway and scooping up the vids before she can ask about them. I toss them into my pocket. I'll trash that crap in a safe spot later. "Sorry if it doesn't look welcoming."

Cat shakes her head. "It's fine. Just...surprising, I guess. Your room is small." She steps daintily over one of my boots and I can't help but notice that both of her feet could fit in there. Kef, I'm huge compared to her. I feel the insane urge to leave my quarters just so she'll have more space. "I can't complain, though. It beats a cage."

"Someone put you in a cage?" My growl reverberates against the ship walls.

She flinches, and I immediately regret it. "Figure of speech," Cat replies in that hard, brittle tone that tells me she doesn't want to talk about it. I make a mental note of it, though. I'm gonna remember. And I'm gonna do something about it. But right now, my female—sorry, Cat—needs clothes.

I turn around in my cramped quarters and activate the wardrobe that I never use. There's a couple of old tunics in here that I got for a gift last Name Day from my mother. They're about three sizes too small because she still thinks I'm a skinny, underfed runt, but they'll do for Cat. "Try these on. I can modify 'em for you if you need."

"Pretty sure I'll need," she tells me, but there's a cheery note to her voice that makes me feel good. I hand her a tunic and she immediately drops the towel and pulls the tunic over her head.

I know she's doped up on pain meds and her ribs are bandaged and she's a mess, but I can't help but realize that her cunt has a little tuft of fur on it. Kef. Now I'm going to be thinking about that tonight when I'm in my bunk. No, I tell myself firmly. She is her own person, and she won't want someone like you. She's lovely and deserves someone better looking, like Alyvos or Sentorr. Or no one. Maybe she wants no one at all, and that should be just fine. She's her own person, just like I told her. "Better?" I ask gruffly, crossing my arms over my chest.

My smallest tunic hangs off her like it's a blanket. The arm holes show her bandages underneath and a hint of her rounded teats. Cat looks thrilled, though. A smile crosses her face and she looks over at me, expectant. "Do you have something I can use as a belt?"

"Imagine I do," I tell her, and turn back to my closet. The ache in my chest is a good thing, I remind myself. It means I've taken her away from those bastards. But still, it isn't right that a female—kef, any creature—should get so delighted at my damned cast off clothing. I fish out a length of cord and offer it to her, and she belts her tunic tighter around her body.

A sigh escapes her and her shoulders sag, and for a moment, it feels like this is the first time she's let herself relax since I met her. Maybe even longer than that. It's like now that she has clothes again and she's clean, she's armored up against the world. "You look tired."

"I am," she admits. "Can I go back to your clinic and lie down?"

"Well, the med-bay's coded to allow anyone on the crew in. I figure if you want privacy, you can have my room. It's a bit of a mess—"

She snorts.

"—But it's programmed to only let me in. I can program it to change that to you and me. No one else."

Cat hugs her torso and she gives me a wary look. "And I suppose you think I can trust you?"

I shrug. "You gotta trust someone."

"No, I don't."

That makes me ache deep inside all over again. "No, I guess you don't. But I'm safe. I bought you for you. Might take some time to get used to that idea, but I won't let any harm come to you. That goes for this crew and for me, too."

She nods and glances around my room. "I can probably find a weapon in here, you know."

"If it makes you feel comfortable, do it." I'm starting to think that anything could be a weapon in her hands and it'd do me no good to try and keep them from her. My bed's more comfortable than the one in med-bay, and she deserves whatever comfort I can give her.

Cat looks skeptical, but I get it. It'll take time for her to realize I mean what I say. "So what about you?"

"What about me?"

"If I'm sleeping in your room, where are you sleeping?"

I grin. "Med-bay."

I wait for her to protest. To say she can sleep there and she's not wanting to impose. That's the polite thing to do. But Cat just nods tiredly, and I remember that this isn't a guest. This is a survivor.

The rules are different.

"Come on," I tell her, moving to the panel on the wall. "Let's get you programmed in here so you can sleep." And I've got to go round up Alyvos, since I'm feeling a bit like pounding some slaver heads and I know he'll be up for a fight.

5

CATRIN

I sleep for what feels like forever. When I wake up, I'm enveloped by a feeling of safety and security. I feel like I can relax.

Then the last vestiges of sleep drop away and I remember where I am. I tense, glancing around the messy room. It's quiet. The door's still sealed. No one's come to bother me while I sleep. Even the clothes I neatly folded and set at the foot of the bed are untouched.

Maybe...maybe the big blue devil wasn't lying. Tarekh, I remind myself. I have to remember his name. I think if he would just fling me down on the bed and have his way with me, it might be better. Then I might know what to expect. It's this uncertainty that's making me a little stir-crazy. I'm both on edge and hopeful for the first time in what feels like forever. Have I landed in a safe place after all? Or is this the calm before the shitstorm?

I ease upright in the bed, biting back a hiss of pain. Truth be told, the awful, biting pain is better than it was yesterday. The numbness is wearing off, but things feel more knitted together, less hot and achy. My face doesn't throb with my pulse anymore. All good things. I look around the room, mentally searching for signs that it's been disturbed while I slept. Before I went to bed, I tried to organize things a little. I cleared off the sleep pallet, folded some of the scattered clothes, and set a few objects in very specific ways so I'd know if someone came in and adjusted things. I'd also searched for hidden cameras and found none.

This morning—if it is morning—everything's undisturbed, though. The long strands of hair I carefully laid on the floor in front of the door remain in place, and the junky piece of equipment I balanced on the edge of a stool right in front of the entryway is unmoved.

Maybe this Tarekh guy is legit.

Oh please, please. I don't think I can take much more.

I shove that desperate thought back, because if I have to take more to survive, I will. I'm never giving up. I get to my feet, stretch a little, and rebelt my tunic. It's the most (and cleanest) clothing I've had in months, so that's a plus. My stomach growls and I decide it's time to emerge from my cocoon and face whatever the universe has in store for me. I've never been good at hiding.

It takes me a moment to figure out how to open the door, but I eventually manage the same careless hand flick over the panel that Tarekh did, and then I'm in the hall of the ship. It's cliché, but it reminds me of every science fiction movie-type ship out there—gray and unwelcoming and just a little dark, with lighting built into the walls. The metal floor underneath my feet is strangely warm, and I tiptoe out, looking for a familiar face.

I round a corner and there's an open entryway that looks like it leads into a break room of some kind. Two of the big blue aliens hunch over tables. One is slurping noodles with some sort of weird tong-like utensil, and the other is holding what looks like an ice pack to his face. Both look up at the sight of me.

I freeze, my senses going on alert.

"Cat," Tarekh says, grinning at me. He puts down his bowl and gets to his feet, and I'm reminded again how big and strong he is. A shiver of fear races down my spine, but I ignore it. There's something about his face that looks different today and as he comes closer, I realize what it is.

He's bruised to hell. His deep blue skin is mottled with even darker bruises, and one eye is swollen shut. It makes his strange features even that much stranger, but he's smiling at me like he won the lottery. I look over and his friend is just as beat up.

"Did I miss something?"

"We won," the other guy says flatly. He gets to his feet, casts a look over at Tarekh, and then leaves the room.

"Won? Won what?" I ask, curious.

Tarekh just shrugs his big shoulders and points at the chair he recently vacated. "Bar fight. Sit and eat. You hungry?"

"Always," I admit. Food is one of those things that I've learned you never overlook. Doesn't matter if it's cooked bugs atop worm noodles, I'm going to slurp it all down because I never know when the next meal is coming. Slaves aren't fed three square from what I've experienced.

I shuffle over to his seat and he pushes his bowl across from me, then moves to the wall and starts punching buttons into a menu. Something in the panel swooshes and then there's a busy hum while a bowl plops out and begins to fill with noodly stuff. He leans against the wall and glances over at me. "Better this morning?"

I nod, pressing my fingers to my face as I keep my gaze glued to that bowl. I'm hungrier than I thought I'd be, and his calm, relaxed manner is making me hopeful that this isn't another trick, that the rug's going to be pulled out from under me again. Surely the universe isn't that cruel. "My face feels better."

"Infection's gone, looks like. I can change your bandages after you eat, get some more numbing agent on it." He grabs the bowl when the last noodle slides in and then picks up a utensil and offers it to me. "Eat first."

I don't have to be told twice. I take the bowl and the comically oversized utensil and start shoving food into my face. If my manners are crap, he doesn't comment on it, just sits across from me and eats his own food. Whatever it is, it's pretty tasty. Kind of like a cross between salt and vinegar potato chips and mushrooms. I'm pretty sure it's the best thing I've eaten in the last year. Maybe ever.

My bowl's empty before I realize it, and my stomach hurts from how much food I've eaten, but I feel good. Relaxed. When Tarekh pushes something that looks like a beaker toward me, I realize it's a drink and sip it. Plain, clean water. Nice. I guzzle it down, too.

Then there's nothing else to eat or drink, and I sit and watch him polish off his own food. It's weird. His features are very foreign to me, and I can't say that he's handsome. But his eyes have crinkles at the corners, which makes me think he smiles a lot, and there's a kindness to his ugly face that has appeal. I remember how carefully he wrapped my ribs yesterday, telling me what he was going to do, and not manhandling me like I was nothing.

There's a lot to be said for small kindnesses.

"So what now?" I ask, hugging my arms to my waist and ignoring the twinge my ribs send up.

He looks over at me. "You want more food?"

Yes, my brain screams, but I ignore it. Pretty sure I'll vomit if I eat more, but instinct's a tough one to ignore. It wasn't what I was asking anyhow. "No, I mean, what happens to me now?"

Tarekh nods slowly, then puts his bowl aside. There's a couple of noodles floating in the broth at the bottom and I have to clasp my hands to keep from snatching them and eating them. God, how did I get like this? "You're safe here," is all Tarekh says. "You don't have to go back to the station unless you want to."

Why on earth would I want to? I shake my head.

"I can't take you back to Earth," he tells me, heading off my next question. "But if you've got someplace else you want to go, you just speak up."

"Am I safe here?"

He nods. "Safe enough. Though I'm gonna be honest—this is a pirate ship. We don't exactly play by the rules. Might be boarded by authorities and locked up at any minute, but we're smarter than that." He grins at me, white fangs flashing. "Long as you don't mind hanging out with lowlifes, you're here for as long as you like."

I think of his friend, the one with the ice pack on his face. He didn't look pleased to see me awake. "The others don't like me."

"Doesn't matter what they think," Tarekh says, leaning back and crossing his arms. His big legs sprawl under the table, and we're sitting so close that practically puts me between them. Is that a hint, I wonder? Is my safety in exchange for sexual favors?

I've had worse deals. If it means food and a bed and no one beating the shit out of me, I'll take it.

"They're outvoted," Tarekh is saying, and that pulls me from my thoughts of bodies and bargaining.

"Outvoted?" I ask.

"Yup. He knows it, too. See, we're a crew, but we vote on things. Sentorr and Alyvos can be pissy all they want, but they know that when the captain and his mate get back, they're outvoted. Fran will vote to keep you, and Kiv's going to do whatever Fran wants." He just gives me an amused little grin. "And of course, I vote to keep you, too."

His smile is so warm and friendly that I don't even mind that his face is kind of patched up badly and his nose is uneven. It sounds like he's protecting me from the others, so I need to stay on his good side. All right, I know how to manage that.

"Thank you," I tell him, and put my hand on one outstretched knee. I rub my thumb over the fabric and lock my eyes to his. "Shall I show you my thanks? Right under this table?" I drop my voice a husky note, because it's all part of the role I need to play to survive—the grateful, horny captive.

He goes stiff and his eyes widen. He leans in and I think he's going to whisper something to me, but he just plucks my hand off his knee and then stands up. "That isn't what this is about."

I watch him, curious. Ever since I was stolen from Earth, I've known what these people want from humans, and it's only one thing. "That's *always* what this is about."

The big alien scrubs a hand down his face and for a moment he looks so consternated that I want to laugh hysterically, because it occurs to me that neither of us knows what to do with the other. "You're safe here," he tells me again.

"With you," I clarify. "But not because of sex?"

"No sex." He heaves out a breath and then begins to pace the room, his tail flicking. The smile's gone from his face and he rubs the base of his horns, as if they feel hot. "And not just me. You're safe here with everyone. If Aly or Sentorr so much as touch a hair on your head, they'll be shitting from a new hole I'll tear in their asses."

Uh huh. I don't entirely believe that. "But I'm not crew."

"Not unless you want a job."

I brighten at that. I can do something besides lie on my back or use my mouth to earn a place here? "Okay, give me a job."

"Really?"

"Really."

6

CATRIN

*T*he job I get is terrible. Actually, it's not just one job, it's several. The *Fool's* an older ship and so there are small things that need to be repaired on a regular basis. There are ducts that need to be unclogged, small wires to be replaced and re-twisted, filters to be changed, and hoses to be un-gunked. All of these can be done by the big blue guys if in a pinch, but they have to dock the ship on an atmosphere-and-grav planet and take it apart to do so, or they can have it serviced for a fee at any station...and then there's a record of the ship and what it had done, which apparently they're not fond of.

Or they can send an alien with small hands and a lean body into the ductwork and have her do those tasks manually.

So yeah, that's my job. Chimney sweep of the stars, or something along those lines. Half of my day for the next week is spent crawling through (barely) human-sized pipes in the walls, shouting at Tarekh with things like, "The blue one or the green one?" and then cleaning things. Lots and lots of cleaning.

I love it, though.

I didn't think I would. It's filthy and sweaty and I've touched horrifyingly dirty things that have left greasy coatings under my fingernails. It's cramped and uncomfortable and I'm really, really fucking good at it.

Or really "keffing" good, as Tarekh and the others would say.

The fact that I'm so eager to work means that I'm learning a lot about the ship—and the crew—on a daily basis. I learn how the filters scrub the oxygen particles and recycle the air. I learn how the water's piped through the ship. I learn how the different pieces are put together and I learn that Tarekh is really, really patient and just as easygoing as he seems. He never gets upset, not even the time I pulled the wrong wire and shut off all the power on the ship and left Sentorr squawking with outrage. Alyvos and Sentorr still aren't quite used to me yet. It's only been a week, but we're still like wary cats being forced to live together for the first time. There's a lot of staring and circling and not much communicating. Tarekh doesn't seem to mind that, though. He says they're just slower to trust and that I'm doing good work. I'm saving them money and earning my spot on the ship.

That makes me happy.

So does the fact that I've been sleeping in Tarekh's room for the last week and no one's tried to barge in. No one's tried to watch me shower, or catch me alone in a dark corner, or anything. No one's hinted that my mouth is better used for things other than talking, or grabbed my ass. I actually am starting to believe that I'm safe here.

It's a feeling that makes me want to cry, just a little. But I don't, because I'm long past the crying.

I throw myself into work instead. The captain and his mate—who is human, apparently, too—still haven't returned from their vacation and so the three remaining crew are busy restocking and servicing the ship while at the station. I start to feel a little more welcome when I see Sentorr checking in supplies in the mess hall and I find out he's ordered an extra box of my favorite noodles. He doesn't smile at me, but I'm the only one that eats that particular kind.

I might get a little weepy thinking about that. After I was taken from Earth, I didn't think I'd ever find a home again. That life would be one endless teeth-gritting round of horrible shit to endure until I died.

Here, it's not so bad. I'm not hungry, I'm not thirsty, I'm not being hit on, and I've got a place. I've got a friend in Tarekh, and I think I can work on the others.

I'm...happy.

It scares me to death.

~

"YOUR HANDS ARE SHAKING TODAY," Tarekh comments from his spot on the floor. "I can hear them smacking against the pipes. How come?"

I shake my head, even though I'm up in the ductwork and he can't see that. "Just thinking. Can you hand me that pointy tool with the little spatula thing on the end? There's some black gunk here over one of the chip slots and I need to scrape it out." I lean down and shove my hand out of the shaft into the med-bay. They're not all that shaky. I'm just...worrying. The captain should be back today or tomorrow, Tarekh says, and I'm afraid that my happy little interlude of this last week might be coming to an abrupt end. He says that the captain's nice and that his human is, too... but what if she's jealous of another human in her territory? I'm going to assume the worst, and that's what makes this hard.

I want to stay and I don't know if I can.

"That black gunk's corrosive. Don't touch it or it'll kef up your skin something awful." A second later, the tool I asked for is slapped into my hand and I get back to work.

"No touching," I tell him cheerfully. "Got it." I slide the flat part of the tool against the crud and start to chip away at it.

"Watch your hands," he tells me again. "If you're too shaky, come down and take a break."

"I'm fine, Mother Hen," I tease him.

"That a human thing? Because my language chip tells me a hen is a fat bird, unless I'm hearing wrong."

I laugh. "Human thing."

"Kind of like the fuck word?"

"Exactly like that. But nothing to do with sex."

Down below, he grunts as I scrape. "Good. I was starting to wonder about humans."

I snort-giggle. "Humans are just as weird—or as normal—as every other sentient being, I think. Sex is always on the brain to a certain extent."

"You're safe here," he tells me unnecessarily once more. It's like he feels he needs to keep saying it just so I know for sure, and that's kind of sweet.

"You might have mentioned that once or twice," I tell him, scraping the last of the gunk into one of the bio-disposal bags, sealing it, and then handing it down to him. I get a glimpse of his big face as I lean over and stick my arms out, and he pulls me out of the duct and back to the floor of the med-bay. "I'm still willing to work for my spot here in any way needed, you know."

"I know," he tells me, and there's irritation on his face. The sight of that no longer sends me into paroxysms of fear, because I've learned that Tarekh is like a big, easygoing teddy bear of a devil-alien. There is absolutely nothing scary about this man other than his size. I even like his ugly mug, though it's less ugly to me as the days go by and more comfortable and appealing. "You tell me that often."

"It's because I want to stay. I know sometimes—"

"No," he says again.

"I can for you," I offer. "I wouldn't mind." And I wouldn't. I've had so much sex—non-con and otherwise—at this point that one more round wouldn't make a difference to me. It'd be like, well, scraping black gunk in a sweaty, hot duct. Necessary to keep my spot.

"No," he says firmly once more and the look on his face is fierce. "Didn't bring you on the ship for that, and I've said it a hundred times already."

And just because he's so indignant, I can't help but tease him a little more. "Not a fan of humans?"

The glare he gives me is quelling. "Not a fan of pity pussy. I've had enough of that in my life, thank you."

Pity pussy? "Why is that?"

He gestures at his face. "This."

"What's 'this'?" I ask, and repeat his gesture. Because I'm not seeing it.

"I am exceptionally ugly even to members of my own people. I'm fine with it. But it doesn't make me popular with the females. You done with that tool?"

I hand it back to him and watch curiously as he stalks away. Ooh, he's in a bad mood. Because he thinks he's ugly? I study his back. From here, he's big and muscular, of course, and intimidating to any kind of human. When he turns around, though, I don't see any particular thing in his features that makes him "more" hideous than the others. Sure, his face is a little messed up from old fights. His nose has been broken and rebroken a bunch of times, but I've seen worse. And if he's scarred up and his eyes don't quite line up? They're still warm and friendly and wonderful and I love it when he smiles.

"Fuck anyone that tells you that you're ugly," I say to him. "I like your face."

He's quiet for a long moment, as if he doesn't know what to say. "Humans do have strange tastes after all."

I just snort at that and open my mouth to respond, but then there's a chime on the overhead intercom. "Captain on board," the ship coos out in a sweet voice.

And then I forget everything we were talking about, because the moment of reckoning has arrived.

7

TAREKH

*C*at's clearly terrified of the captain.

Kinda hilarious in theory, because if she knew the guy, she'd realize there was absolutely nothing to be afraid of. Kivian's more likely to hold her down and adjust her hem than to hurt her.

But after a week of being around my Cat, I know that her fears are because she's been treated badly in the past, and it makes me want to protect her. So when she goes pale and moves closer to me, I put a hand on her neck and give her a comforting squeeze of reassurance. "You're safe," I repeat to her again. At some point she's going to start believing it.

"I'd feel safer if you'd let me—"

"Nope," I say before she can finish. She keeps offering up sexual favors and I can't take 'em. It makes my spirit wither a little each time she does, because I know that's how she had to survive ever since she was taken from her planet. She's a tough little thing, though. Doesn't talk about it. Doesn't cry over it. She just grits her teeth and does what needs to be done.

Someday maybe she'll tell me what happened. I suspect it'll make me sick, but if she needs to speak about it, I'm here for her. Really, I'm just here for her in whatever way she might need me.

Even if it's just as a friend.

There's no denying I've had dreams about her. No denying I've grabbed a bottle of lubricant from one of the med-bay drawers and stroked my cock to the thought of her touching me. Of her looking at me with need in her eyes instead of that strangely dead expression she gets when she offers to suck my cock. But I know it'll never be. She's had a bad past and I'm an ugly cuss. It ain't a great combo, and I'm happy to be her friend and defender. She hasn't had many of those in the past and I aim to pick up the slack.

"No need to worry," I reassure her. "The captain isn't going to mind."

"But he doesn't know I'm here," Cat argues, worried. "You guys said you're already one human over your four-man crew. What if—"

"One more human won't matter. They don't eat much." I give her neck a squeeze. "Come on. You can say hi to the captain and his mate. I think you'll like Fran."

She doesn't reply, so I gently steer her forward, keeping my hand clamped on her shoulder in case she tries to run away. Or more like she tries to attack the captain. That seems more likely.

"Honey, we're home," Fran calls from somewhere down one of the halls. "Where is everyone?"

I can hear Sentorr respond from the direction of the bridge. "Tarekh's got a bit of a surprise for you."

"Uh oh," Kivian says, but there's laughter in his voice. There usually is. That's one thing that makes him such a good captain to work for—he takes everything as a joke and never lets things stress him out. I've got a very similar philosophy, so we get along well.

Poor Cat doesn't realize that about the captain, though, and she's stiff as I push her along. It's obvious that she's worried.

"It'll be fine," I murmur to her. "Trust me."

"You promise?" she whispers.

"Promise," I agree. After I say that, the tightness in her shoulders eases.

I guide her to the bridge—though after a week of being on the ship, she knows where it is by now. All the others are already gathered there, including Kivian and Fran. The dark-haired human is wearing a simple gray jumper that I've seen on szzt ship crews, but they're the closest in size to humans and so she has a whole wardrobe of them. In contrast, her mate is dressed in the latest fashion from Homeworld, with slab-sleeves that consist of layer upon layer of fabric and ties, geometric patterns on the hem of his tunic, and plas-leather boots that go up to his knees. He looks ridiculous, but then again, he knows that. I'm not entirely sure if it's an act with him or if he really likes the clothes, but he does his best to overdress for every occasion.

Everyone turns at the sight of us, and I keep my hand clasped on Cat's shoulder so she doesn't bolt. "Meet our newest crewmember," I say, as if it's no big deal.

Fran's jaw drops. Her eyes go wide and I see for the first time the minute differences between the two of them. Fran's skin is more of a golden color, her mane long and black, her eyes dark. Cat's coloring is lighter, her hair a tan sort of shade that I've only seen on rare woods, and her eyes are gray-blue and pale. Of the two females, Fran has larger teats and a taller frame, whereas Cat is small and lean everywhere. It makes her look far more breakable —or maybe it's just because I know Fran better and know how tough she is.

"Oh my god," Fran says as she moves forward, her arms out. She envelops Cat in a hug, squeezing her tight. Or trying to. It's clear from Cat's stiff-armed response that she's not used to the touching. Cat gives me a helpless look but endures the embrace as Fran rubs her back. "Another human! It's been so long since I've seen another face like mine!"

"Not counting Chloe," Kivian adds.

"Not counting Chloe," Fran agrees, stepping backward. She gives Cat another little smile and then looks over at me. Her expression darkens and she steps between me and Cat. "You bought a fucking human? I'm going to murder you, Tarekh—"

Cat quickly slips out from behind Fran's back and steps in front of me, her arms wide. She's protecting me.

A funny ache starts in my chest.

"Don't get mad at Tarekh," Cat says, her voice twice as fierce as anything I've ever heard. "He bought me to save me. He took me here and patched up my wounds and he hasn't so much as touched me. He says I can be crew if I earn my keep."

Sentorr and Alyvos are both looking at me with narrowed eyes. Kivian's just giving me a sly look that makes my horns get hot at the base. "Didn't buy her for sex," I say. "Thought that should be obvious." I cross my arms over my chest and try to seem casual even though I'm secretly a little worried that the others won't accept her. "She was hurt pretty bad. Couldn't leave it be."

The look in Fran's eyes gets soft and she pats Cat's shoulders. "I'm not going to hurt him. Stand down." Cat doesn't move, even when Fran smiles at her. "And of course you can be crew! I'd love to have another human on board."

"As captain of this vessel, don't I get a say?" Kivian asks, amused.

"No," says Fran.

Kivian barks a laugh, throwing his head back. "Ah, my sweet mate, you are delightful. Of course she can be crew. More humans will make this place a lot prettier than looking at these ugly faces." He gestures at the rest of us.

To my surprise, Cat scowls at Kivian. "Quit saying that. Tarekh's not ugly."

I'm torn between astonishment and wanting to squeeze the small human against my chest. Such an ardent defender. "I'm lucky to have someone so fierce on my side," I tell her, pleased.

"Do we even get a vote?" Alyvos asks, looking decidedly less pleased than the captain and Fran at the thought of another human.

"Why?" Kivian leans against one of the control panels and crosses his boots at the ankle. "Fran, me and Tarekh are all voting against you."

"Fran shouldn't get a vote. She's biased." Aly scowls. "She—"

Kivian's laughing mood is gone. "Watch yourself," he says quietly.

Alyvos goes quiet. He shakes his head and then retreats back to the bridge. Fran exchanges a look with Kivian, but she tries to hug Cat again, anyhow.

"He'll get used to it," is all Kivian says. "Don't concern yourselves. I know I'm not going to."

It's settled, just like I knew it would be. Cat's gonna be the sixth crewmember in a four-person ship. Crowded, but not unheard of.

Sentorr rocks back on his heels, face implacable. "So what now? Do we stay and get modifications for the *Fool*? Open up part of the cargo bay for a chamber for the human or—"

"Cat can have my room." I keep my voice mild even though I don't like 'the human' comment tossed in there. I'll have a word with Sentorr later. "I'll keep sleeping in the med-bay."

Fran makes an exclamation of surprise. "You're sleeping there? I'm surprised you can find a table under all your mess in there."

I shrug. It's not the most comfortable place—some of that my own doing—but I like the thought of Cat nice, safe and snug in my bed. Don't wanna change that.

"We're not staying," Kivian adds. "Bit of a problem with one of the locals. We should probably head out." He pauses for a moment. "And change our name. And our call signal. And our records."

Sentorr groans, because that work falls on him. "What did you do?"

Fran just shakes her head.

Kivian looks indignant. "He insulted my mate. What I supposed to do?"

"Not ram the head of a kaskri bigwig into a wall?" Fran says sweetly. She puts a hand on Cat's shoulders. "Come on. I have some clothes that should fit you. It'll be more comfortable than that tunic you're wearing. I'm assuming it's Tarekh's?"

Cat gives me a reluctant look as Fran tries to lead her away, and that funny feeling starts in my chest again. I'm not used to someone looking at me like I'm the only bright spot in their world, the only person they trust. Normally my ugly mug scares everyone away.

Tarekh's not ugly, Cat told them defiantly.

I nod at her encouragingly and then she goes with Fran. Ah, kef. She's going to be the death of me, I think, because I'm already wrapped around her small human fingers and she doesn't even realize it.

"So what's our new name if it's not the *Dancing Fool*?" Sentorr asks, annoyance stamped through his demeanor.

"How about the *Lovesick Fool*?" Kivian smirks in my direction.

I make a rude gesture back at him.

8

CATRIN

*F*ran is...nice. I think.

It feels like it's been so long since I've been around another human I'm not really sure how to act. She's very huggy and keeps putting her arms around me, which is awkward. I don't want to hurt her feelings, though, because she's clearly happy to see me. The hardest part is that my brain is telling me to trust her because she's human, and it's been a long, long time since I've been able to trust anyone...except Tarekh. Part of me wishes he was here. Doesn't matter if I'm changing clothes. I don't have anything he hasn't seen before.

I think.

Fran chats a mile a minute as she leads me into what must be the room she shares with the captain. Seeing as how this is a pirate ship, I thought it'd be more...piratey. Instead, it's pretty luxurious, with gauzy, colorful wall hangings and artistic vases and lots of decorative pillows on the bed. And when Fran goes to the wall and flicks her hand over the terminal, a massive closet shoots out. She gives me a wry look. "Most of these clothes are Kivian's. Mine are in this small drawer down here." She pulls it out and there's a neat row of tightly folded tunics in a bunch of different colors. "I'm all about utility, but that man loves his fashion." She shakes her head. "So what colors do you want? Green? Blue? Green number two? Blue number two? The szzt aren't the most originally dressed race, but the jumpers are decent. No panties, though."

I blink at her, trying to make sense of how easy she is. How happy. She's not like me, I don't think. I feel like I'm nothing but scar tissue at this point, growing back all hard and ugly. Surviving, but the tough way. Clothing colors seem like such a trivial sort of thing when you didn't have clothing that covered everything for months on end.

But that's in the past. I don't want to think about the past ever again. It's dead.

"Your coloring is a lot fairer than mine," she says, grabbing a few tunics in a paler green. "These will probably look better on you than me."

"Thank you," I remember to say after a moment.

"So, where are you from?" she asks, and then pauses because the intercom chimes overhead.

"Darling, I'm afraid we have a bit of an issue," Kivian says over the speakers.

Fran sighs and rolls her eyes. "We were followed, weren't we? You said we wouldn't be."

"It appears that I might have overestimated. Could you be a gem and take our newest crewmember into the safety chamber and hide there until I give the all clear? We're about to be boarded by the port authority."

"On it. Love you." Fran kneels down on the floor and lowers her body, reaching for something behind the artful wooden desk.

"Love you, too, my precious one."

"That man," Fran says with a huff, but I think she's pleased. There's a low "snick" and then the massive wall panel that shows a sunset scene flips outward, revealing a small, brightly lit chamber inside. Gray, smooth shipping crates are stacked along each side, but there's enough room for both Fran and me. I notice she picks up a gun from the closet and stuffs it into her belt before heading toward the room. "Hopefully this won't take too long."

TWO HOURS LATER, we're still sitting in the small, stuffy room. Fran taps her feet impatiently, but I just sit there, clutching my new clothes. Fran doesn't seem worried despite the fact that this is taking a while, so I take my cue from her. If she's not concerned, I'm not. It is, however, getting a little hot. I wipe at my brow and wiggle a bead of sweat off the tip of my nose.

"I know," she whispers. "It's hot. We can't have any ductwork on the schematics, though, or we'd get discovered for sure." She leans back against one of the crates. "I hate this part, but it's necessary. Haal Ui isn't the type of place to give a shit about a couple of contraband humans, but if Kiv asks me to hide, I do it, no questions asked. I tell myself I'm protecting the cargo." She pats the crates and gives me a smile. "It's definitely a strange life, but you get used to it."

I nod. From my experience, humans are treated a lot like exotic monkeys. Some people like to fuck the monkeys, unfortunately, as I've found out. There's deviants in every corner of society, I suppose, even the space ones. I don't mind hiding, though, as long as it means I don't have to go back to my last owner. "How long have you been with the crew?" I ask.

"Over a year now, I think? Human year, that is. The mesakkah one's different and I can't ever figure it out." She shrugs. "I mostly gauge time from job to job. That's all that matters to me."

"Are you...happy?" It seems such a weird thing to ask, but I can't help myself.

Fran's dark eyes consider me. "You mean here in outer space, surrounded by aliens, never to return home? Yeah, I am. At first I was hoping that Kiv and the others would take me back, but then I realized even if I got home, I'd never be the same person I was. That all changed overnight. So I put those thoughts aside and once I did, it was easy to fit in. And I love Kivian." Her soft smile tells me more than her simple words do. "He's impossible, of course. I've never met such a big, strong, tough guy who's also into fancy sleeves and fussy art, but he is. I love that he's so much his own person, and I love that he's never seen me as anything but my own person, too. That's rare out here."

I know what she means. So many times I've been treated like a walking, talking dog. Or a vagina. When someone treats you like a person, it matters.

Kind of like how Tarekh's always treated me. I think of how quickly everyone was to accuse him of doing something nefarious with me and I feel the need to defend him. "Tarekh's been wonderful to me," I tell her. "I was scared at first, but he's never put a hand on me. I think he genuinely wanted to help someone that was hurt."

"Oh, Tarekh is absolutely the best," Fran agrees. "He's got the kindest heart. But don't kid yourself that his motives were a hundred percent pure."

"What do you mean?" I suddenly feel cold with worry.

"Not like that," Fran says, catching my look. She raises her hands in the air. "You don't have a thing to worry about from Tarekh other than possibly being buried in all the trash in his room. That man's a slob to end all slobs. I meant that I saw the way he looks at you. He adores you already and I'm guessing he'd do anything for you. He won't ever touch you, of course. That's not who he is. But that doesn't mean he can't love you from afar."

I snort. Love me from afar? Please. I think of the big lug and how he's always teasing me or joking around. "We're just friends."

"I know. Which is why you're totally safe. He knows it's not meant to be."

And that makes me wonder. Why is everyone so certain that Tarekh can never score with anyone? Not that I'm looking for romance. I'm not looking for anything except to have my bed— and my body—to myself for a while. But I feel bad that everyone discounts Tarekh, who's a great guy. "Why do you say that?"

She shrugs. "By mesakkah standards, he's what we would call 'damn ugly.' I've seen women at the cantinas cringe if he smiles at them. He's huge, too, which doesn't help. Some of the mesakkah are pretty vain and all of them are good looking, so I think it must really suck to be an ugly one." She shrugs. "You'll never find anyone with a better heart, though."

I think of Tarekh. His broad, open face. His smashed-and-repaired nose. The messed-up plates on his forehead and the way they make his eyes look slightly uneven. His big, easygoing smile. His scars. He's not pretty, no. But he's so appealing I can't imagine how no one can see past that. He'd make some girl a great boyfriend. Mate. Whatever. Poor guy. These people are assholes if they're too shallow to see past an imperfect nose and facial symmetry. Fuck them. "I like his face," I tell her stubbornly.

Fran just smiles. "So what are your plans, Cat? You're welcome to stay here with us, of course, but not everyone wants to spend the rest of their days on a tiny pirate ship with four big blue brutes. I'd completely understand if you wanted to go somewhere else."

I shrug. "As long as it's safe here, I don't much care. Like you said, I take it from day to day." I've had to for a while—for all the wrong reasons—and trying to think of the future, like I might actually have one, hurts my brain.

"Well, we can take you anywhere but Earth, I imagine." She pats the crates. "We've got to dump a shipment of these unregistered blackmatter crystals a few starsystems away. That'll take a couple of months because we need to take a few backwater traffic lanes, so to speak, to avoid authorities. Once we get those out the door and get paid, we're free to take you to a different planet, or starsystem, or wherever you'd like to go...except Earth."

"I see."

"Kivian's brother also married a human, you know. They live on a little farm planet out in the boonies. It's quiet, but that far out in space, no one much cares if you're illegal. You could probably stay with them for a while if you wanted to get away from this life."

"I'll think about it," I tell her. For now, I want to stay here. Tarekh's my friend, and I don't abandon friends. They're too precious to come by, just like safety. As long as I'm welcome here and no one's hurting me, this is as good a place as any.

Besides, I have months before I have to make a decision, it sounds like. Plenty of time for a girl to change her mind.

9

CATRIN

Two Months Later

THAT DIRTY RAT.

I snort when I push the dispenser in the mess hall and dark blue lotara noodles come out instead of my favorite askri noodles. The salty askri noodles are a particular favorite of one other person around here who knows we're weeks away from getting another shipment, and who knows I'd lose my shit if I found out he ate my supply.

Tarekh is so going to get it. Like I wouldn't know that he stole my noodles? The lotara are dark blue and askri have a greenish yellow tinge to them because they're so salty. That dick. Of course, I picture Tarekh eating the last of them late at night with a gleeful look on his big face and then loading a different kind just to fuck with me and see my reaction. That's totally something he'd do. I can't stop grinning as I stop the dispenser mid-noodle and pull my wrench out of the toolbelt that's slung low on my hips in Han Solo-style.

Tarekh thinks he's gonna get away with this, huh?

Ten minutes later, I've pried the panel off of the food dispenser and put soap into Tarekh's next favorite noodle type. Just one serving, of course, because I'm not about to waste a bucketload of food, but he'll see what it's like when you fuck with a girl's noodles. I put the panel back on, push my wrench into my belt once more, and then decide that instead of eating, maybe I'll go mess with my favorite medic a bit more.

As I head out of the mess hall, Alyvos heads in. "Don't eat the jirri noodles," I warn him. "They're booby-trapped."

"Kef me. Are you two playing games with the noodles again?" He groans. "You realize it's against military procedures to tamper with the food supply?"

I make a face, mimicking his words, and he makes a rude gesture at me, which I promptly make back. I've learned that these guys can be a little gruff, but they're also predictable and nice in their own way. Alyvos is still hung up on his military service. Sentorr's obsessed with making the ship run like it should. And Kivian— well, Kivian's the party boy. Tarekh's the heart of this place, the peacemaker. Fran's the mom, I guess, if there has to be a mom.

Me? I'm not sure what I am yet. Family dog, maybe. I can live with that. All I know is that I love the *Lovesick Fool* and its crew and the last two months have been pretty keffing great, all things considered. I'm safe. I've got friends. I'm useful. Sentorr's even been teaching me how to shoot a blaster in case we get boarded. Even though Sentorr and Alyvos were both salty at the thought of me joining the crew, we get along great now. They treat me like a kid sister. Fran's my female best friend, Kivian's...well, he's just Kivian.

As for me and Tarekh, it's kind of a weird relationship. Something more than friends, something less than...more. We needle each other constantly. We push each other's buttons. We know how the other person's mind works and he's the only one that can make me laugh so hard that I nearly pee on myself with delight. He's the best thing on this ship, hands down, and everything on this ship is pretty fucking amazing.

I bite my lip so I don't whistle a tune as I head towards the med-bay. I'm going to surprise that dork and let him know that I'm on to his noodle games. I'll say one thing about Tarekh, he never lets things get dull. I'm grinning even though he sabotaged my noodles, just because I know he must have been planning this for a while. He's going to want to see the look on my face—

As I stand outside the med-bay, I hear a low groan and then my name, whispered on a breath.

Goosebumps skitter up my arms. I know what that sound is. I recognize the voice, and he's speaking low enough that he doesn't want anyone to hear. This is supposed to be secret. I should be freaking out right now that our platonic, comfortable friendship has taken a weird turn. I should turn around and leave.

Instead, I hit the override on the door panel and manually crack open the door to the med-bay so I can watch.

From my vantage point in the hallway, I can see Tarekh's strong, broad back. His muscles flex and his tail lashes back and forth. He's shirtless, the tattoos on his body and his armored plating a subtle, beautiful dance over his skin. I've seen him like this before, of course, because when we're doing the dirty work on the ship, he tends to strip down or else his clothing gets messed up. I get it. I've destroyed more sleeves and ripped more holes in my jumpers than I care to think about.

I'm more interested in the fact that his trousers are loose around his waist, and his ass is tight, his hand pumping in front of him furiously. The other hand grips the wall and his head is bent, his horns in the air.

And I just barely hear my name breathed again.

Again, the goosebumps cover me, but I don't feel alarmed or freaked out. Strangely enough, I'm...flattered? Pleased? It's weird. I haven't thought about sex since I got here on the *Fool*, because I didn't want to. It's been almost two months and I'm starting to feel like a normal person again, not a toy to be used and discarded. I haven't thought about my past because I've put it behind me. It's done and I'm moving forward, even if it still haunts me in my dreams every now and then. But looking at his beautiful back and the way every cord of muscle in his body is clenched toward release, I feel a stirring in the pit of my belly. A yearning.

I remember what good sex was like.

I remember how good it felt to have your partner's weight lying on top of you, and feeling so sexy and gloriously wonderful as he pushed between your thighs so deep it felt as if you were one. I remember the intimacy of it, the connection.

For the first time in a long, long time, I miss that.

Tarekh's head snaps back and he lets out a harsh little grunt, and his shoulders heave. He's coming. I think for a flash and then slide the door shut again without a sound. Just as quickly, I re-activate the panel and slide my hand over it. "Crewmember Cat incoming," the computer chimes.

Tarekh curses and grabs an old tunic, shoving it over his crotch as

I saunter in the room, clearly the best actress in the world. I don't show a hint of what I just saw and smirk at him instead. "Oh, don't cover that shit up," I tease. "Like I haven't seen that before."

He just rolls his eyes at me, keeps the tunic in front of his cock, and heads toward the water-closet to wash up.

I hop up on the med-bay bed and let my legs swing back and forth while I wait on him. I didn't miss the slight flush of deep color at the base of his horns—the mesakkah version of blushing. I didn't get to see his cock, though, which is a little disappointing. I find myself curious as to what it looks like—what he looks like. I've (unfortunately) had my share of alien sex, but never with one of his race. For a moment, I'm glad. I want him to be the first.

Then I wonder why the hell that thought popped into my mind. I'm not having sex with Tarekh. We're just friends.

But then I think of how he said my name while he stroked his cock. Just letting off steam, maybe? Perhaps I'm the only female to jerk off to other than Fran and she's married?

Thinking of Fran reminds me of what she told me when I first joined the crew. *Doesn't mean he can't love you from afar.*

I thought she was full of shit. Now I wonder.

Tarekh returns a few moments later, his pants fastened and his belt in place. He gives me a half-snarl that doesn't scare me as he saunters past. "You should learn to keffing ask if it's safe to come in."

"You should keffing learn not to stroke your wang during daylight hours," I retort, though I'm secretly pleased. I think of the husky little way he said my name. God, I liked that far too much. What is wrong with me? I swing my legs, a mixture of anxious and amped up. Something about catching him in the act like that has changed everything, but I'm not quite sure what it is.

He just grunts at me, pretending to be surly, and goes to his inventory panel on the computer, pretending to check shit out. "What do you want?"

"Someone ate all my noodles in the mess hall," I say lightly. "Don't suppose you know who that is?"

Tarekh just glances over his shoulder at me and a sly grin curves his mouth. It's like a punch to the gut, that clever little smile of his, and I'm left breathless with how handsome he is. No, I decide. Not handsome. He'll never be handsome by anyone's standards, and I'm fine with that. But there's no denying he's appealing. It's his personality, his strength, and his playful mind. His protectiveness when it comes toward me, and his utter contentment to just be my friend if that's all I want.

Doesn't mean he can't love you from afar.

Oh god, I'm not sure I want to just be friends anymore. I'm so confused.

"Wasn't me," he says, and it takes me a moment to realize we're still talking about noodles. Seems funny to do so when my world's changed in the space of a few minutes. The noodles were before I caught him secretly rubbing one out in my name. Tonight, I'm probably going to do the same, just to see how it feels.

The thought makes my pussy clench, and I cross my legs, pressing my thighs tightly together. "What are you up to?" I ask, changing topics.

He grunts. "Inventory."

"Like you can find anything in this pig pen," I tease, reaching out with one foot to nudge his swishing tail. I keep cleaning up after him in here and he keeps messing it up again. The man thrives in chaos, which is kind of cute—no, funny. It's funny.

Cute is for boyfriends. He's not my boyfriend.

Doesn't mean he can't love you from afar.

Arrrrgh.

"You look restless," he tells me, tapping a button on the panel before glancing back over at me.

I don't tell him that he's the cause of my restlessness. I'm not that brave and I haven't sorted my own head out yet. I watch his tail swish back and forth, showing the agitation he won't, and decide a different tactic. "Thinking about other planets and what I'm going to do once we finish this blackmatter run."

He turns and looks at me fully for the first time since I came in the room. "Oh? You're not staying on the *Fool*?"

"No, I think I am," I say quickly. "But I'm just thinking about options."

Tarekh nods and picks up a pack of plas-wraps. "Smart. I've been a lot of places. You can ask me about 'em if you want. Tell you what I know."

"Tell me about Homeworld," I say, curious about the main planet his people hail from. I know from talking to the crew that the mesakkah have spread to other planets, but most still say they're from Homeworld or are only a generation or so removed. There's a lot of cultural pride surrounding that place from what I can tell.

"What do you want to know about it?" He puts a big hand to the back of his neck and rubs, tilting his head back and forth in a way that I find fascinating. I can't stop staring.

Damn it, why are all of his movements suddenly fascinating? Just because I caught him jerking his dick? What the fuck is wrong with me? I shake my head to clear it. "So they all look like you there, right?"

He chuckles and tosses the rolls of bandages into an open cabinet, and they bounce right back out. "Not if they're lucky."

For some reason, that irritates me. I hate it when he calls himself ugly, as if having a pretty face is the only virtue a person can have. "Well, then I don't want to go there."

Tarekh gets really still. He blinks and then looks back over at me. The mesakkah can't move their brows, but I've learned to interpret the set of his mouth and it's clear he's a little perplexed. "Are you...flirting with me, Cat?"

Flirting? Flirting???

He sounds so astonished that the vehement denial on my lips changes to something else. "What if I am?"

The big lug just rubs his jaw. "Don't mind me saying, but you can do better."

Grr. "Maybe I don't want to. Ever think of that?" My heart's racing. I don't have a single idea of where I'm taking this conversation. All I know is that I don't want him to think that I find him ugly. Never that. Never.

Instead of looking pleased or flattered, or even surprised, his expression grows distant. His expressive mouth flattens and I can tell he's pissed. That tail whips in the same direction twice before flicking in the opposite direction like an angry cat. "I thought we went over this. You don't need to fuck me—or anyone else on this ship—out of gratitude. You earn your place with work. You don't have to earn it on your back."

Anger explodes in my mind and I leap off of the med-bay bed. "How fucking dare you?"

His eyes go wide at my fury. Tarekh reaches for me. "What? I'm just saying—"

I shove at him with both my hands, palms on his warm, fuzzy chest. God, I hate how even that feels nice. "You fucking fucker. You think that's something I'd really do? After my past? After the last two months? You think I'd just pity fuck you because hey, what's one more dick and Tarekh could use a good lay? Fuck you." I shove past him and slide away before he can grab me to stop me. "FUUUUCK!" I yell at the top of my lungs and slam a fist into the wall as I storm out of the med-bay.

That fucking asshole. Pity fuck indeed. So much for flirting with the guy. I'm so mad I could scream.

I do. Again. Just because it feels good to snarl at the universe.

Then I storm into my room—that used to be Tarekh's—and lock him out of the door override so he can't disturb me.

10

TAREKH

Cat's vehement reaction surprises me. Why is she so mad?

I'm still rattled and recovering from the fact that she caught me jerking off. She acted like it was nothing, but a few moments earlier and she would have heard me groaning her name. I don't want her to know that I'm obsessed with her. That I've considered her mine ever since she tried to stab me in med-bay with my own needle. She's not interested in me like that, so it's just another thing I'll bury deep and smile through. That she's safe and happy is enough for me.

My heart, anyway. Maybe not my cock, but my heart for sure.

Her flirty offer just makes things worse, though. Because I want to say yes to what she's suggesting, more than anything. But I also know it's wrong. Not only because she's not ready, but because she doesn't feel the same way I do. If she touches me, I don't want to see that dead look in her eyes. The "I'm going to endure this because I have to" expression I've seen on whores. I want her to touch me because she wants me as bad as I want her, or it's no good.

And I know she'll never want me like that.

Fran jogs down the hall, a confused look on her face. She glances over at me as she passes med-bay. "What's eating Cat?"

"She's fine," I say.

Now Fran gives me an incredulous look. "She's cursing at the top of her lungs. What about that tells you that she's fine?"

I shrug. "Okay, she's mad at me. Either way, it's fine."

Fran looks down the hall, as if determining whether or not to go after Cat, and then turns to me. "What did you say to her?"

I can feel my horns getting hot. Just a little. "Ain't nothing. I might have suggested something that pissed her off."

She smirks. "She found out you ate all her noodles?"

I rub at my bald head. "Er, no, not exactly. I mean, she did, but that's not what she's mad about." I wonder if I should keep it a secret, but then again, Fran's human. She'll know what I did wrong if it's a human sort of thing versus a Cat sort of thing. "Can I talk to you a second?"

"Of course." She follows me into med-bay and kicks aside one of my old tunics. "God, you're a slob. Didn't Cat just tidy this place up for you?"

I shrug. She might have. "She likes to annoy me with shit like that."

"More like she likes to look after you," Fran says, crossing her arms over her chest and leaning back against the wall in a move so much like Kivian I'd laugh if I wasn't so confused at the moment.

"Look after me?"

"Of course. Out of all of us, you're the one she's closest to. She gets along with the boys and me, but it's you that she turns to for everything. You haven't noticed that?"

I've seen Cat straightening up, of course. Within a few days, she had my wreck of a room all cleaned out and tidy. Figured she just liked neatness and nagging me, and that's why she's always getting in my space and picking up my clutter. Thought she was just picking at me and making sure people knew she had value.

But from the way Fran's smirking at me, I think I'm wrong.

"She was flirting with me, I think," I admit. "And I might have told her I didn't want her pity."

Fran smacks her forehead with the palm of her hand, and a heavy sense of dread settles in my gut. "You keffing idiot!" she exclaims.

"What?"

"She likes you."

I'm perplexed. "Of course she likes me. We are friends.

"No, you dweeb. She *likes* you."

This must be one of those translation things. "Explain."

Fran rolls her eyes. "I can't believe you're so obtuse. Okay, let me spell it out for you. She's your shadow around the ship. She gets along with everyone, but she spends her time with you. You two have this weird little thing going on that we've all noticed. Like the noodle games."

"It is because we are friends—"

"So you do the same to Aly and Sentorr? To Kiv? To me?"

I frown, because of course not. They would not react the same as Cat would. Aly would snarl, Sentorr would sputter. Kivian would laugh, and Fran probably would, too. Only Cat would get this wild gleam in her eyes and decide how best to take revenge on me. I admit that's my favorite reaction. I live to see her smiles. "None of that means anything."

"Riiiight. And how about when she gets mad when you say you're ugly? Or if Aly makes a crack about it? She always corrects him and gets mad."

She does. In fact, nothing makes Cat madder than someone insulting me, even as a joke. I'm so used to it I pay no mind—I *am* ugly—but it makes Cat furious. "It is because she is sweet."

This time, Fran snorts. "She's about as sweet as a badger. Trust me when I say you're blind. Oh, and an idiot."

The reality of what Fran is saying hits me. Does Cat...wish to mate with me? Not out of pity but because she feels something more? I do not know what to do. I have never had such a problem before. Females usually avoid my company. Cat is different, though. She is...well, perfect. "What do I do?"

"Talk to her?"

Talking is good. I think. For some reason, I feel nervous. For all her fierce attitude, Cat is fragile in both body and spirit. A male must tread carefully around her because I want nothing more than her happiness, even if it means ignoring my own.

Fran is right. I should talk to her. If nothing else, so I can find out if she truly does like me, and what happens next. At this moment,

I think Cat does not like me very much at all. Perhaps it is already too late.

CAT DOES NOT COME out of her chamber—my chamber—all afternoon. She doesn't respond when I knock, and when I send her messages through the comm system, they go unread.

Stubborn human.

When she doesn't come out for dinner—and I find the soap in mine—I decide it's time we talk. I head to her door and knock again. She doesn't respond, so I move to one of the air ducts and call up, "If you don't let me in, I'm going to remove the door to your room. I have all my tools."

That gets her attention. A moment later, the door to my old chamber opens and she scowls at me. "I'm flashing back to my high school days, so thanks for that."

I have no idea what she is talking about. "I wish to speak privately with you."

"That's funny, because I have nothing to say." Her shoulders are stiff, her arms crossed, and it's clear her feelings are still hurt. She stands in the doorway defiantly, as if daring me to push her aside.

I feel like a cretin. "I did not wish to hurt you, Cat. May I come in so we can talk?"

She shrugs and moves aside, heading to the bed.

My room has always been one of the smaller chambers on the ship, but I never minded it because I had no reason to hide away, and med-bay to go to if I needed space. Here, though, it looks perfect for Cat...and yet as I look around, I cannot help but notice she has kept all my things. The bed is covered with my blankets, the wall-screen set to my favorite scene. A shelf has been programmed into one of the flex-walls and she has set up all of my tools and gadgets in neat, clean rows. I imagine that if I pull out the closet, I'll see all of my clothing. It's all still me even though she's living here. I'm both humbled and a little troubled by it. So much stuff and none of it is Cat's. Is it because she's not planning on staying? My heart clenches at the thought.

She moves back to the bed and curls up against the headrest, her delicate legs tucked under her. Cat looks so pretty and fragile that I want to sit next to her and hug her close and make her worries go away. But I can't do that, so I look around for someplace else to sit instead. The room is so clean that I can see the floor for the first time in what feels like forever, and there's a low stool in the opposite corner that I forgot I had. I grab it and pull it forward, then sit across from Cat. "I wanted to say I'm sorry."

It's clear that wasn't what she was expecting to hear. Her head tilts and she blinks at me. "You're apologizing? Why? I'm the one that messed up."

"You didn't mess up." I scratch at my scalp, then shift in my seat. She's makin' me all nervous. I can feel my tail flicking back and forth. "I just...you know. Thought you were offering because we're getting close to the station and you were worried you weren't gonna be able to stay."

"Oh. No." Her two words are sour.

I'm keffing up this apology, too. I need to say what's really on my mind, even though the words are hard to spit out. "See, ah...it's like this." I rub my jaw. Rub it again. I'm a big male, but confessing how I feel to this small female is harder than anything I've ever done. "Most females think I'm ugly—"

"You're not ugly," Cat retorts vehemently.

I raise a hand. "I know you don't think so, and I think that's part of the reason why I have a hard time believing someone as perfect as you would flirt with someone as ugly as me." When she opens her mouth again, I shake my head. "Let me go on, because this needs sayin' and I don't think I can say it twice."

She gets quiet, hugging one of the pillows to her chest. It's almost as big as she is.

I rub a hand over the bristle of my scalp again. "I've mated with females before, see. If you've got money and you've got a cock, you're bound to buy a bit of cunt in-between runs. Back when I was a soldier, and then after that. Most of the females you run into on those stations will do whatever you want for a few credits. They're always eager...until they see me. They take one look at my face and jack up the price, or decide they're too busy, or they take the money anyhow and then just 'endure.' I can tell by the looks on their faces and the way they avert their eyes that they're doing their best not to look at me. At this." I gesture at my face. "When I was a young kit fresh in the military, I told myself I didn't care. That my money was good and I could pay for cunt even if normal females wouldn't look in my direction. But then I bedded one after coming home from the war and..." I shake my head. "She didn't look at me. And when I was done, she got up and started scrubbing herself so hard you'd have thought I was covered in filth. Realized then that only one of us was having a good time. Told myself after that that I'd keep my cock to myself and never push myself on another female, even if there was money involved."

"That pisses me off."

I look up, surprised. Here I've been pouring my heart out to her, admitting my most shameful experiences, and that's what she has to say? "What does?"

"Why does everyone act like you're a keffing leper? So your face is a little messed up. That doesn't mean that you're not an amazing person. People are such assholes." She punches the pillow and then scoots to the edge of the bed. "Are any of these women at the station we're going to? If so, you need to point them out to me so I can beat their heads in."

I can't help but smile a little at that. "So fierce. I'm flattered, but it's not necessary, Cat. I'm not telling you that so you can feel sorry for me—"

She makes an outraged sound.

"Right. No feeling sorry for each other. Just wanted to say if I came across as rude and hurt your feelings, it's because I was rattled after you caught me. Felt exposed. Didn't know what to think." I scrub my hand over my head again. "Didn't want you to feel pressured into doing something you didn't want to do. I'm not that kind of male."

"You think I haven't figured that out yet? I can see 'that kind of male' coming from a mile away at this point. I've had a lot of experience with them. That's why I feel safe around you." Her expression gets shy. "That's why I like you."

"You do?" I feel a warm rush of pleasure at her soft words. Pleasure...and astonishment. Out of all the males on this craft, she likes me? Alyvos and Sentorr are both far more attractive.

"Don't sound so shocked. And I think I do." She bites her lip. "I'm actually not sure. That sounds terrible, doesn't it?"

"No. I understand." Because I know her. I can guess at what happened to her on the station and I know she's struggled to trust. I've seen her fighting with her fear and in my eyes, she's incredibly brave. Of course she's scared and unsure. I would never hold that against her. I get it. I'd be surprised if she wasn't. "You don't have to explain yourself to me."

"No?" she asks, and her voice is half-amusement. "I don't know, sometimes I think my head is so messed up from what I've been through that I'll never be normal, and then sometimes all I think is I need a few quiet hours to rub one out, like you did."

I'm shocked at her words...and my cock gets hard immediately. I force myself to ignore it and shift in my seat. "Can I ask...what happened to you back on the station? I don't mean details. I just want to know how you got there...but only if you want to tell me."

Cat shrugs and hugs her knees to her chest. "I can talk about it, I think. But I'd prefer if it just stayed between us."

"Of course." I'm humbled she'd trust me enough to confide in. "I would never tell."

She nods, her expression thoughtful. "It almost feels like it all happened to another person, a long time ago. That I've always been here on the *Fool* with you guys, and all that other stuff just happened in a movie to someone else. Except sometimes I dream it and I remember it was me." She shudders.

I hate her pain. "You don't have to talk about it—"

"No, I do," she says, interrupting me. "If you and I are ever going to be anything, if we ever want to be anything, you have to know." But she won't look at me. Her gaze grows distant.

Then, she begins to talk, and part of me wishes I'd never asked. The things she describes are so awful, so degrading that it makes me ill. Her story starts out the same as Fran's—she was taken from her bed one night—and then soon devolves into a nightmare. Unlike Fran, she wasn't rescued days in. She was sold to a whoremaster on Haal Ui and forced to survive. She tells me everything, even when I no longer want to hear.

I picture my delicate, fiery Cat in the horrors she describes in that flat voice and it makes me angry. Furious. I have to clench my fists so I don't shake with rage. Instead, I force myself to keep listening because once she's started talking about it, she can't seem to stop. She tells me about every awful customer she can remember, every person that hit her or slapped her—or worse. She tells me everything.

Everything.

Part of me wonders if she's telling me every sordid detail because she wants to scare me off. The opposite is happening. I feel more protective of her with every moment that passes, and I vow to myself that even if I have to die—or take everyone in this universe down with me—she's never going to know that life again. She's going to live the rest of her days safe and happy.

"And then," she says with a tiny shrug. "I met you."

"I remember," I say, and get to my feet. "Thank you for telling me."

Cat looks a little surprised. "You're leaving? Where are you going?"

I crack my knuckles like Alyvos does. "I have to go punch things."

11

CATRIN

I'm told by the others that Tarekh demolishes every crate in the cargo bay. Not just the wood ones from the primitive planets, but the sturdy plas ones from the more "civilized" trading federations. He punches and destroys so many things that Alyvos gets concerned and tries to stop him, and also gets punched in the face. Hours later, when Tarekh is done, he retreats to med-bay and wraps his knuckles up with healing film and numbing gel.

The others are mystified at his actions. Tarekh's the nice one, the gentle one. They don't understand.

Me, I feel warm inside.

I get it. He smashed everything he could because he couldn't hurt those that hurt me. I should be upset, but I'm fucked up in the head because it makes me happy. He's the only one I've told what I've been through. He's the only one I ever plan on telling. And his reaction makes me feel less alone, weirdly enough. Like someone else gets it and understands me.

Still, I can't help but worry when he doesn't come back to my chamber that he's thought long and hard and decided against wanting me. That I'm too dirty and used for him. That even ugly mesakkah have standards. Doubt and worry gnaw at me and I can't go to sleep even when the hour grows late and the rest of the crew heads off to their beds except Sentorr, who stays on the bridge because the man has no life.

I lie in my bed and think about Tarekh.

Actually, I guess I'm lying in Tarekh's bed. He's still sleeping in med-bay, where it's uncomfortable and sterile. He says he doesn't mind. I've offered to switch with him, but he refuses. Says I need my privacy. Maybe I do, but tonight, I kind of wish he was here with me, even if it terrifies me to think that. The crew of the *Fool* is so small that any ripple in the social dynamic feels huge. Heck, it's been two months and Kivian still complains that Aly and Sentorr are grumpy that I'm here. What if Tarekh and I try to take things to the next level and I can't? Will he hate me?

I don't know. I hate that I don't know. I want there to be answers instead of just more questions.

I stare at the door to my room. Should I get up and head over to med-bay? Talk to Tarekh? See how his hands are? Or am I too chicken?

I...might be too chicken. I roll over in bed and move to the wall panel, where the controls are easily in reach for the central comm. I don't recognize the alphabet on the keys—mesakkah written language is lower on my list of things to learn—but Tarekh helpfully colored the keys that I need to dial him in med-bay. We've communicated back and forth before, but never after bedtime. It feels a little more intimate this way, but not as intimate as a face-to-face meeting would be.

I tap the buttons and wait for him to answer.

Tarekh picks up immediately, surprising me. He's still awake. "You okay, Cat?" There's concern in his gruff voice. "You don't have the vid screen on."

"I know." Mostly because I don't want to stare at his face right now. I'm feeling too fragile. "And I'm okay." I hesitate, because I wanted to check in on him and instead he's worrying over me. "Are we good?"

There's a pause. "Are you asking if I feel different than I did earlier?"

I swallow hard. "Yeah."

"Cat, I think you're my favorite person I've ever met. Nothing that you told me changed that."

I swallow the knot in my throat. "Thanks."

"Are *you* good?"

"I don't know," I admit. "I don't know how I feel about any of this. I'm just worried..."

"That something will change and we won't be friends any longer?"

I'm torn between laughing and crying. Laughing because he knows me so well and crying because he's exactly right and I'm terrified. I'm frightened I'll send mixed signals or the flirting will go too far and then I'll want to stop and he won't and then everything will get ugly. I've always told myself that when others touched me, it was just sex. A bodily function, no more than farting or burping. Thinking about it in crude ways helped me distance myself from what was happening.

But I know that if I touched Tarekh and he touched me, it'd be different. Those mental boundaries would be gone. Maybe that's what scares me most of all.

"You'll never lose me as a friend, Cat. I promise." His voice is warm, slightly rough, but so good I want to use it as a blanket and wrap myself in it. "I'm here if you want me. I'm here if you don't. I'm here if you change your mind about all of this and just want a buddy. And I'm here if you want more. There's no pressure."

"Okay," I breathe. Some of the tightness in my chest eases. "Thank you."

I want to say "I love you," but I don't know if that's just my messed-up head or what. So I end the comm before I can do something I regret.

If Tarekh says things are safe, I believe him. If he says he's going to be my friend no matter what, maybe...maybe I test that. See how it feels to be more than friends. I kind of like that idea. I hug my pillow close and go to sleep, imagining that my bed isn't empty and a big blue alien's curled up next to me, his body protectively sheltering mine.

I sleep better than I have in years.

12

CATRIN

*F*or the next few weeks, I push things out of my comfort zone. The teasing in our relationship is kicked up a notch and it turns into something sexy, flirty. I'm the one that takes the lead in everything, because I know Tarekh is giving me my space to figure things out.

He's also got the patience of a saint, because I don't make it easy for him. I'm determined to toe the invisible line between us, to see how far I can take things and still feel safe. I keep waiting for him to snap, for him to grab when he should just admire. For him to destroy the fun playfulness between us.

But he never does.

I know it's wrong to tease him like I do. I know I'm playing with fire, waiting for it to burn me so I can go back to how things were. Maybe that's why I start coming out of the ducts legs first, so he has to grab my ass to help me down. Maybe that's why I call the med-bay every night and whisper sexy things to him, just because I like to hear his muffled groans.

Maybe that's why I get brave enough to send him an audio file of me masturbating.

Everything I do pushes just that much further. And every time Tarekh responds with patience and that same wonderful, charming amusement that rocks me to my core, I fall a little more in love with the guy.

I'm not ready to make a move yet. I know I'm going to have to be the one to make that first move. Not because he's afraid to—but because he doesn't want to push me. Because he knows what I've been through and knows I might take a lot longer than most girls to respond to a kiss or a caress...or that I might never respond again.

We'll see. At some point, either he'll break or I will, and I don't think it'll be him. He's not impatient like me. He's the most patient man I've ever met.

Which means I just have to try harder. Which is kind of fun when you know that you're safe.

13

TAREKH

*T*hat human female is going to kill me.

I grab my cock in my hand while in the water closet and give it a fierce tug. It doesn't take much to make me come these days. All I have to do is imagine Cat smirking up at me as she teases the zip down the front of her tunic a little lower so her teats practically spill out when she leans over in the mess hall. Or I listen to that audio file she sent me, the one I've already listened to so many times that it's permanently ingrained in my mind. Or I think of the sexy little gasp she made when I accidentally brushed up against her in the hall...and how she deliberately stopped so she could rub up against me again.

She's a cruel little thing and I love it.

Cat's games are making me wild with need. I love the boldness that's come out of her over the last few weeks as we head toward Rii Ketta, another distant station several galaxies away. It's not as seedy as Haal Ui, but it's still not what I'd call classy by any means. I'm a little worried about what's going to happen when we get to the station. Is Cat going to leave? Is someone going to give her shit when we're there? I feel incredibly protective of her.

Of course, I also want to kef her brains out. But her security comes first.

That's why I don't touch no matter how much she torments me. That's why I rush back to med-bay to tug my own cock several times a day. It's either that or do something we'd both regret, and I'm not about to scare her. Bad enough that I have this big ugly face and hulking body. I'm not going to do a single thing that will make her bad memories resurface. I like seeing happy, flirty Cat far too much. My whole world changes the moment she walks into a room, and to think that a male like me is lucky enough to have her attention is humbling.

I won't do anything to put that at risk.

Just thinking about her is enough to make me spill with a few jerks of my wrist, and then I stand in the spray of water, washing away my seed and taking deep breaths.

Sentorr's calm voice comes over the comm. "Rii Ketta in sight. Docking shortly."

I bite back my growl of frustration. It's too soon. What if Cat decides to stay? I'll smile and be happy for her, but everything inside me will die. I wouldn't stop her, but I wouldn't be the same if she left.

But if it's what she needs, I'll make sure she gets it.

By the time I emerge from med-bay a short time later, I'm fully dressed in a ship uniform of *The Distance*, which I think was a water hauler, given the logo over my pocket. Fits pretty good, and if there's any misbehaving, it doesn't follow me back to the *Fool*.

Kivian comes down the hall, adjusting his fussy sleeves. He's dressed in a new outfit bedecked with baubles at the hem and more folds in his sleeves than an entire fleet of mesakkah fashion models would wear. Fran just rolls her eyes with amusement when I look over at her. In contrast to her mate's ornate clothing, she's wearing a simple pale green jumpsuit, zipped up to the neck.

It makes me think of Cat and how she unzipped hers, showing skin. I start to sweat a little more.

The others are on the bridge, but all I see is Cat. She's dressed in a pale pink, filmy sort of tunic that glimmers when she turns. It makes me think that it's something Fran's held into for a while, waiting for the right moment to wear it. It suits Cat and her pale coloring, and the sight of her makes my mouth dry with want. Cat has her face close to the port screens as if they're real windows. She's staring out at the slowly spinning diamond that's Rii Ketta. I'm drawn toward her and notice that the hand she has clamped down on the rail is trembling a little.

I bet she's scared. Excited, yes, but scared. We've been in a little bubble for months, making this long-haul delivery. Haven't had to think about the outside world or anyone other than the people on this ship. I brush my fingers over hers and she looks up at me, a faint smile on her face. "I've never seen a space station. I guess I've been in a few, but I never got a chance to look..." She pauses and then glances over at me again. "Are they all so pretty?"

"Pretty on the outside, same old shit on the inside," I tell her cheerfully. "Nothing to worry over."

She smiles at me, but she doesn't look convinced.

"Well," Kiv says and clasps his hands together. "We about ready to go? Our buyer won't be here until tomorrow, so tonight's all about enjoying ourselves. That means refreshment dispensers, music, and an open tab at the cantina." He rubs his hands together with glee. "Maybe even a few rounds of sticks."

"Just don't bet anything you'll regret this time, love," Fran tells him, bumping her hip against his gently. His tail immediately curls around her waist.

"What about the humans?" I ask, because it doesn't seem fair for the rest of us to escape the confines of the *Fool* for a while and them to be stuck on board. If that's the case, I'm staying at Cat's side. I wouldn't leave her.

Fran pulls a bright metal collar out of her pocket and snaps it around her neck, handing Kivian the decorative chain. "Arf arf," she jokes, pretending to be some human animal. "Got one for Cat, too, if she wants to play along. It's the easiest way to have no questions asked and stops you from being messed with." Fran pulls out the second collar and holds it out to Cat. "If you'd rather stay on the ship, that's fine, too. You and Sentorr can hang out."

Sentorr just mutters something about peace and quiet.

Cat takes the collar, fingering it lightly. It's on the tip of my tongue to tell Fran that the collar is a bad idea, that it's going to give Cat bad memories. That she doesn't need something so humiliating, even as a disguise. That she's all dressed up and so pretty we shouldn't ruin tonight for her. But then Cat snaps the collar around her neck and hands me the chain. "Wanna be my owner?"

My mouth goes dry. "You...sure?"

Her eyes flare with that flirty heat. "Might be fun."

"Cat, you could have a safe word," Fran suggests. "If things get too much for you, just speak it out loud and someone can take you back to the ship."

"A safe word," she muses, fingering the collar on her neck. "That's a good idea. Something human?"

Fran says, "That works."

Cat gives me another playful look and I feel like I'm about to break into another cold sweat. "Leather daddy?"

Fran snorts.

"What is that?" I ask.

"A man that ties his woman up and gags her for fun." She shrugs and holds the end of the chain out to me. When I take it, our fingers brush and I can feel her trembling again.

"Let's pick a different word," I suggest. Something less fraught with sexual meaning. Something that won't scare her by thinking about it. Because Cat is fragile and even now, I want to protect her with everything I am.

Cat gazes up at me with those unusual human eyes and then just smiles. "Sandwich, then."

14

CATRIN

I'm glad Fran suggested the collars.

My first instinct was to flick it out of her hand. To knock it to the floor and stomp it to a million pieces. No one would blame me. But she's in the same boat as I am—she knows how humans are looked at on these kinds of stations. To aliens, we're walking, talking sex dolls. People don't think anything of grabbing a girl or invading her personal space. They just don't care. We're not real people to them.

So a collar is smart. Insulting, but smart. I can be attached to an owner and no one's going to mess with me at all.

I give my chain to Tarekh. Of course I do. Sentorr's a loner and prefers to spend his time on the ship instead of partying on the station. Kivian has Fran. Alyvos is nice enough, but he's not Tarekh. When I hand the chain over to the big medic, it feels...sexy.

Like things just went up a notch between us.

Like we just silently agreed to take things to the next level.

We didn't, of course, but it feels that way. Maybe it's the fun, shimmery pink dress-like tunic I'm wearing, or maybe it's that to the rest of the universe, I'm now known as Tarekh's woman. Either way, I'm feeling a little excited as we enter the station and walk with the crowds, but no one thinks a thing of a human female clutching at the belt of a big, brutal mesakkah pirate. They might give us a second glance, but no one reaches out to touch me. And I'm free to hang off Tarekh as much as I want. I can hold on to his tail or slide my hand into the crook of his elbow. I can put my hand around his waist and snuggle up to him and everyone in our group will think we're just pretending. Everyone on the station will think I'm his pet.

Either way, it's all completely safe.

I love that. Even though I have a collar around my neck, it feels strangely like freedom to be here with him like this. I glance over at Fran and she's lightly holding on to one of the ties on Kivian's sleeves as we wind our way into the station. Alyvos saunters at the front of the group, and Tarekh and I make up the rear.

The air smells a little funky on a station. I'd forgotten how much it smells like a public restroom. There's a faint stink mixed with antiseptic cleaners, and it makes me wrinkle my nose and I realize how crowded the station is. There are people everywhere, and the low hum of voices trading, laughing, and yelling at each other is overwhelming after months on a quiet ship. I move just a little closer to Tarekh. He puts one big hand on my shoulder and for some reason, that feels so comfortable and welcome that I want to cry.

Instead, I just give his tail a little tug.

Tarekh stiffens, his eyes going wide, and I send him an innocent smile.

He grabs my hand. "Not that, not in public." The base of his horns are deep, deep blue and I suspect I might have just made a faux pas. He never tells me no, but the look on his face is nothing short of shocked.

Okay, no tail grabbing in public. "Got it." I slide my hand back into his belt. His fingers brush over my hair and then he settles his palm on my shoulder once more.

Under his protective grip, I notice that while people might stare, no one's grabbing or touching. That's completely different than my last station experience, when, if I was upright, anyone would feel free to grab and pinch anywhere and everywhere. I decide I like this a lot better, even if it means I have to wear a stupid collar. Faint music starts to pulse through the hallways, and then we're heading toward a place that must be the local cantina.

The cantina is crowded with people of every shape and color. I'm pretty sure I see something that looks like an overgrown frog in a codpiece walk past, talking with something humanish that's orange and pebbly looking. On the stage, a girl with four spindly arms and a gigantic, bouncy butt shakes her moneymaker while others play sticks at tables and bubbles of opalescent fluid float in the air.

Wow. I feel a lot like Princess Leia in a *Star Wars* movie, right down to the collar.

"Table at the back," Alyvos calls out over the crowd, and pushes his way through the cluster of people. We follow, and this time Tarekh pushes me in front of him, both hands on my shoulders. Someone eyes me appreciatively and glances up at Tarekh...and then quickly hurries away again. I'm guessing he's glaring at them.

I think I like that. A lot.

We settle in at the table, and some things don't change. Like at an Earth diner, the table's a long booth with a curving seat around a tiny table with multiple stations. I'm amused to watch the big mesakkah aliens squeeze in at the table, since it's clearly made for people slightly smaller than them. Of course, Fran and I look like little kids, my chin barely reaching the table top and my feet not touching the ground. It's a little ridiculous.

I find myself seated next to Alyvos, with Tarekh on the other side of me. "Comfortable?" Tarekh asks, dropping my chain discreetly between us.

"I guess?" I put my chin on the tabletop as a joke and find it sticky. Ugh. Joke backfired. "As long as I don't have to see what I'm eating or drinking, I'm cool."

He frowns, looking concerned.

"It's a joke, big guy. Whatever they're serving, I'm sure I've eaten worse."

But he just rubs his chin. "I'm not sure if the food here's been filtered for humans. There might be indigestible elements that could cause a problem for your system."

Fran pulls something out of her pouch. "I brought snacks from the ship for us humans." She gives me an apologetic look and hands me a plas-wrapped package. "I've run into this sort of thing before. Trust me when it's better not to try the food. If you value your guts, don't do it."

Yeesh. I take the squares from her. "Maybe I should have stayed on the ship with Sentorr."

Tarekh tenses next to me. "You want me to take you back?"

I shake my head. Truth is, I'm kind of enjoying this. It's been months since I've left the ship and I didn't realize how much I'd enjoy a change of pace. The music's weird, the food's apparently inedible, but it's nice to just kind of kick back and relax. I watch Kivian slide an ornately sleeved arm around Fran's shoulders and she snuggles up against him, and I feel a pang of longing. I want that.

I look over at Tarekh and he's just watching me, his eyes soft with affection. My heart squeezes at the sight, and I smile at him. I adore this man.

Kivian reaches over to the center of the table and hits a toggle. The table lights up, reading bio signatures, and the refreshment dispensers begin to whirr. I'm enchanted by the sight of the colorful bubbles floating into the air. I love that this is the way people have drinks in outer space. So fun. I'm envious that I can't drink one. "We should get one of these back on the ship," I tell Tarekh.

"We should," he agrees. "I'll program one to shoot bubbles for you with stuff humans can drink."

"That works." I look speculatively over at him as a waitress prowls past with a tray of something that looks like chocolate truffles. If I've learned anything about outer space foods, it's that those are probably not truffle-like in the slightest. That helps ease the chocolate urge, just a little. I'm more interested in watching Tarekh, though. "Are you going to drink?"

"Me? Nah." He leans back in the booth and shakes his head. "I'll keep you company on the no-drinking policy."

"Aw. But these bubbles are so pretty." I nudge one toward him with a fingertip. "You can drink them on my behalf."

"Maybe." He shrugs.

"Should we try to find some sticks games around here?" Kivian asks, lifting Fran's hand to his mouth and nibbling on her fingertips. "Or just enjoy the company of our females?"

Our females? I'm a little surprised to hear that, but no one can deny that I belong with Tarekh. Even now, I've moved closer to him than to Alyvos, our thighs touching under the table. I have the insane urge to slide my hand between his legs and see what I can get away with here in the throbbing madness of the cantina, but then I remember the tail touch from earlier. Maybe he's not in the mood for that sort of thing tonight.

I glance over at him and his horns are bright blue at the base. Then again...

Alyvos snorts and gets out of the booth, stepping onto the table and pushing aside the refreshment bubbles floating in the air around us. "I'm going to go find someone to fight." He hops off the table and disappears into the crowd. I like Aly, but he's a prickly one to get to know. Seems weird that he wants to start a fight instead of hang out, though.

"Did we do something wrong?" I ask Tarekh quietly.

My alien just rubs the base of his horns and gives me an odd look. "It's nothing to worry over. He, ah." He rubs his head again, and I can practically hear the bristle of his shaved scalp. "He likes brawling for bets. It's his way of unwinding. Releasing pent-up tension."

I wonder what Alyvos is so tense about. I glance over at Fran and Kivian, but they're lost in their own little world, eyes locked. I glance over at Tarekh again, and he's staring pointedly ahead at nothing in particular, that weird, uncomfortable look on his face.

Is he...shy? Did Aly leave because this felt like a double date and he was a third wheel? And Tarekh knows it? Why do I find that so cute? I put my hand on his thigh and smile up at him. "You're not going to abandon me, are you?"

I watch his throat work, and he shakes his head after a moment. "Never."

15

CATRIN

*O*ur eyes meet and the breath catches in my throat. His expression is so soulful, so full of yearning that it hurts me. I want more than anything to reach over and kiss him, but—

"Oh, isn't that cute! Is she a human?"

I look over at the waitress pausing at our table and mentally curse that Tarekh gave me one of those translator chips, because I can't tune her out. I scowl at her cooing voice. She looks taken aback at my foul mood, raising one segmented arm to her carapaced chest.

"She is," Tarekh says mildly. His hand slides to my thigh, and I'm not sure if he's reassuring me or holding me back. "Thought there weren't rules against them here on Rii Ketta."

"There's not." She moves her mandibles in something that might be a smile. "I thought I'd ask if you want refreshment bubbles for the humans at your table? There's a special brew we keep on hand for pets."

"That'd be nice. Cat?"

Pets. I'm still stuck on "pets." Just the word makes my jaw clench. She keeps looking at Tarekh like he can answer for me. I glance over at Fran, but she's just amused, as if she's run into this sort of thing before. I have, too, but it still bugs me. I snap my teeth at the waitress.

She gasps and takes a step backward, looking uncertainly in my direction. "Tame?"

"Or just as sentient as anyone else," I tell her in a too-sweet voice.

She simply blinks at me and then pats Tarekh on the shoulder. "I'll get that pet bubbler for you." She saunters away, swaying her hips in a way that's supposed to be sexy, I guess. For a bug-alien. I guess.

I scowl at her retreating back. "I hate that sort of thing."

"You get used to it," Fran says in a tired voice. "That's why I stick with the people I know and don't much care about anyone else."

"We'll scandalize all of them," Kivian promises her. "Watch me break seven sanitary laws in a single swoop, my pet." He pulls her wrist to his mouth and licks it sensuously. "Done."

"You're crazy," she teases him, but she's breathless and smiling.

"A lovesick fool, perhaps?"

The entire table groans. Tarekh nods at the waitress as she returns and delicately slides a new bubbler onto the table. He hands her something that looks like an iridescent square and she drops it into her cleavage and disappears again. "Don't get angry at her, Cat," Tarekh says a moment later. "She's just trying to shake down a few more credits for the night. She's not interested in me." His mouth twitches with amusement, as if the very thought is absurd.

I arch an eyebrow at him. I hope we're not going to get into the whole "I'm not attractive" conversation again, because he's always wrong. I love his face, and his body. He might not do it for others, but they don't matter, because he does it for me. I glance over at Fran and Kivian, but they're lost in each other, their affection growing more public by the moment. No wonder Alyvos high-tailed it out of here. I nudge the bubbler toward Tarekh. "Show me how to turn it on."

He swipes his finger over a panel, pinches something else, and then a bubble emerges, floating into the air. Aw, man. Human bubbles are boring. It looks like the world's dullest soap bubble instead of the beautiful works of art that are the other drinks. With a sigh, I pull one toward me and taste it. Bitter, too. I make a face. "Pass."

"I'm sorry. This hasn't been a great night for you, has it?" Tarekh rubs my back.

It really hasn't, but looking over at him, I see a way to make it better. I give him a speculative glance and then hitch a leg over him, sliding into his lap. "Night's still young," I tell him with a wiggle. Now I'm straddling him, my back to his chest, my pink skirts spread over both of us, and I glance over my shoulder to see how he reacts.

The look on his face is completely blank. Not excited, not mad, just blank. Underneath my butt, though, I can feel that he's anything but emotionless at the moment. His cock is making its presence known, and I nudge another bubble from the dispenser toward me, drinking it despite the bitterness. Kinda tastes like beer, now that I think about it. It'll do.

Fran just gives me a little smirk as she picks up a card and studies it. "This the menu, babe?"

Kivian shrugs. "Would you like to live dangerously, little one? I can order you something."

"Not me. I've got bars. But you should eat something. You've been talking about those plant-ball things for weeks now. What are they?"

"Avaashi," Tarekh says, shifting under me. It's like a slow earthquake, tilting me back and forth. I wiggle my hips back against him, re-settling myself, and I can't resist rubbing up against his cock, just to see how it feels. To see if I like it or if it sends a bucketload of bad memories through my head.

It feels good, though. Better than good. I bite my lip and flex my hips, pressing back against him to add to the friction, and I hear his subtle intake of breath between beats of the music. "You guys should order some," I suggest. "We can watch you eat and live vicariously through you."

"Unless it looks like cheesecake," Fran says. "If it does, I'm having some regardless of what it does to my stomach."

I laugh, and I'm about to agree with her when I feel Tarekh's big hand on my thigh. That distracts me and I pretend to study the bubbler while I wait to see what he does with it. Is he going to touch me more? Or was that just an accidental brush of his hand and he's going to move it away? Or is he about to push me off his lap?

His hand clenches on my thigh, holding me there, and then he begins to rub his thumb back and forth, as if it's my skin he's touching and not the material of my tunic. Heat flutters through my belly at that small caress and I decide to push things a little further. I grind down against him, rocking my hips in tune to the weird, lilting music of the cantina. "This tune's kinda catchy," I say lightly. "Don't you think, Tarekh?"

"Quickly becoming one of my favorites," I hear him say. His other palm settles on my opposite thigh and he rubs me up and down. Nothing tense or awkward about it, just a slow, easy rub.

It's making me wild with need.

Fran and Kivian aren't paying attention to us, murmuring something to each other as they study the menu. That's good, because I'm getting crazy turned on and I'm pretty sure it's showing on my face. The cock I'm sitting on is a hard bar of enticing iron against my pussy, and every little twitch I make reminds me that I haven't had good sex in a really, really long time. I haven't wanted to for forever, but with Tarekh touching me? Oh, I *want*.

I want bad.

I give him another playful wiggle and I love that his tail shudders on the seat next to us. I know how it feels. I want to—

"You sellin' rounds?"

I stop in my pleasurable rocking up against Tarekh's cock, panting and breathless. I can feel my nipples hard and rubbing against the silky fabric of my tunic, and I'm barely aware of the alien that's come up to our table. I'm very, very aware of Tarekh's deadly growl of response, though, because I feel it ripple all the way through me and it sends another delightful tremor through my body. "You talking to me?" Tarekh asks.

"Either of you," the alien says. I don't recognize what he is. Something greenish and unpleasant looking. He glances between me and Fran. "I'll buy a round with either human. Never had one before. Heard they've got the tightest cunts—"

Kivian jumps to his feet, in the alien's face, rage on his features. I can feel Tarekh stiff underneath me, and I suspect it's taking everything he has not to jump up and do the same. He carefully lifts me up off of his lap and sets me down atop the table. "Be right back, love," he murmurs to me and brushes his lips over my brow as he stands.

Just that tiny touch fills me with longing. I'm hot and bothered and suddenly the club's too much. I don't want to be here anymore. I watch as Tarekh grabs the alien by the throat and growls angry things at him for insulting me. I think of when he beat up my old master and think this guy's gonna get a round of blue fists in his face, too. It's sweet.

But I'd rather Tarekh just take me home and kiss me.

So I reach out and grab at his wildly thrashing tail, sliding my hand over it in a caress.

Tarekh stops. His big frame openly *shudders* and he drops the alien. Kivian immediately grabs the stranger by his collar, hauling him away from us while Tarekh turns to me with an incredulous look on his face that's half outrage, half heat.

I just lick my lips and give him a look of longing. "Take me back to the ship?"

"You've had enough?" He looks worried.

I play with the chain of my collar and give him my best sultry look. "No. I just want to be alone with you. In our room."

The base of his horns grows so dark they look purple in the smoky lights of the cantina. But his eyes gleam with want, and he scoops me up into his arms. "See you back at the ship," he tells Fran and Kivian.

"Bye," Fran says with a wave, then laughs. "Have fun."

Oh, I plan on it. I definitely plan on it. I shiver and press my thighs together even as Tarekh carries me, cuddled against his chest like I'm the most precious thing on this station. I've waited long enough. Tonight's our night.

As if Tarekh can read my thoughts, he leans in and murmurs to me as we pass through the crowd in the cantina. "You sure, little Cat?"

"I'm sure," I tell him, and reach up and trace a finger along the edge of his ear. His entire body shudders again and he gives me a look of such intense longing that I wish we were at the ship right here, right now.

I must be crazy for making us wait so long. It seemed like a good idea until now, when all I want to do is strip off my clothes and fling myself at Tarekh. I loop my arms around his neck and rest my head on his shoulder with a sigh. "Hope you know a shortcut back."

16

TAREKH

a docked ship has never seemed so far away.

By the time I carry Cat over the threshold of the *Lovesick Fool*, I'm pretty sure everyone on Rii Ketta has seen the enormous cockstand I'm sporting in my trou. It isn't helped by the fact that Cat keeps rubbing my chest with her hand and murmuring naughty things in my ear. It's like she knows how crazy she makes me and she wants to push me that much further.

Little tease. I love it.

Sentorr emerges from the bridge, a curious look on his face. He's got his blaster in his hand. "You're back already? What's the problem?"

"No problem," I tell him, and I can feel my face get hot. "We just, uh, wanted to come back early."

Cat gives a throaty little giggle that makes my cock even harder.

Sentorr's expression changes from confusion to mild embarrassment. "Right. Of course." He clears his throat and continues in a stuffy voice. "If you need anything, I'll be on the bridge. As usual."

"Got it." I feel just as uncomfortable as he does, I imagine.

He gives a crisp nod and then disappears.

"I think we just made Sentorr really, really uncomfortable," I murmur to Cat.

"He'll get over it," she tells me, completely unconcerned. Her hand skims over my chest again. "Can I take the collar off now?"

"Yup." I'm ashamed I didn't think of it earlier. "I'm sorry about it."

"Don't be. As disguises go, it's a good one." She unclasps it and then tosses it down the hall. "Just glad that it's nothing more than a disguise."

"Me, too." I stand in the hall with her in my arms, and for the first time since grabbing her, I'm hit with uncertainty. Maybe she doesn't want to go forward. If she doesn't, I'm good with that. "Where do you want to go?"

The look she gives me is achingly sweet. Her arms go around my neck. "Your bed. My room."

I groan. Sweeter words were never spoken.

It's a short distance to my old room—now hers—and when I automatically swipe a hand over the sensor, it lets me in. It takes me a moment to realize what that means. When she got mad at me, she locked me out and I let her. At some point between now and then, she's reprogrammed it to let me in again...which means that all those times she was hiding behind this wall, touching herself, I could have stormed in and joined her.

Just makes my cock harder. Little tease. She's incredible.

My old room is neat, the bed made, and yet she's still managed to keep all my shit. Even more than that, she's managed to make it look tidy and attractive. "You know, I never thought this room would fit one person your size, much less mine."

"There's plenty of room in here for two," she tells me. "Your bed is plenty big."

So it is. I move toward it and gently lay her down on the blankets, because she's the most gorgeous thing I've ever seen and I'm worried my big hands are going to somehow crush her. "You're beautiful, Cat. You know that? You deserve better than me—"

She puts her hand over my mouth, smiling up at me. "There's no one better than you. Don't say such things." When I try to interrupt her again, Cat shakes her head. "When you saw me, all covered in wounds and infected out there in the tunnels of Haal Ui, do you think people were beating each other aside to come rescue me? Do you know how many people passed by me without a second look? Stepped over me? No one cared but you." Her hand slides lower, to my heart. "No one's as good a man as you, and that's why I love you. That's also why I'm terrified of fucking this up."

"Whatever you need," I tell her, "You'll have it. If you're not ready for this—if you're never ready for this, I understand."

"I might not be ready, but that doesn't mean I don't want to try," Cat tells me, and her voice is as sweet as her touch. "I've wanted you for weeks now, but I've been too scared to go forward. I'm tired of being scared. I'm tired of letting the past rule me. I want *us*. You and me, together."

"I want that, too." I'm shaking with how much I want her. I want to grab her and crush her against my chest. I want to taste her soft skin. I want to learn her body...and I'm still terrified of touching her and giving her bad memories. "Tell me where you want to begin."

Cat gives me a thoughtful look. "We could start with a kiss."

A kiss. I know what that is. It's the weird, mouth-on-mouth thing that I see Fran and Kiv doing sometimes. At first I thought it was a strange human custom—even a slightly disgusting one—but now with Cat in front of me, her pretty pink lips parted, I want to try.

Kef, do I want to try.

I put my hand on her cheek, and she looks up at me with such trust in her eyes, a smile on her face. It's as if I'm the one with the terrible past, not her. I can't get over how perfect she is, how brave. How loving. I'm not worthy of her, but I'll do everything I can to make her happy. Starting right now.

I lean in and press my mouth to hers gently, feeling awkward and wondering if I'm doing it right. If it's pleasing her. I want to get this right.

Her laughter brushes over my face and she pulls back, grinning at me. "It's a kiss, not an execution."

"It was bad, then? Is there a trick to it that I'm missing?"

"Yeah, the trick is to have fun." And then she flings her arms around my neck and presses her lips to mine with such intensity that I'm taken aback. A moment later, her tongue pushes into my mouth and then she's stroking it against mine and I've never felt anything so amazing. Forbidden, yes, but amazing. Now I know why Kivian gleefully breaks hygiene laws with his Fran. It's because putting a mouth atop another mouth feels like...mating, but with tongues instead of cock. She puts a hand to my jaw, her other arm looping around my neck, and continues to kiss me, her mouth slanting over mine as her tongue flicks and teases against my own. I can't get enough, and so when she breaks away, panting, I let her catch her breath and then immediately take over the kiss. This time, I'm the one plunging my tongue against hers, mating her mouth with mine, claiming her lips.

I'm doing it right, too, because she moans and rubs her teats up against me. "Just like that," she breathes. "You have a nice mouth."

I want to tell her that she has a nice mouth, too. That her smooth little tongue flicking against mine is making me wild. But words mean I have to use my face for something other than pleasuring her, and there's no time for that.

Of course, if putting my mouth on her feels this good already, I can't wait to put it on all of her. I'm too impatient to pace myself and begin to kiss my way down her jaw and neck, pressing my lips against her soft, oddly colored skin. I love the little sounds she makes, and the way she grabs on to my horns, as if she can't get enough of me, either.

This is what I've been missing in the past. This is why matings from long ago felt wrong and ugly. It was because there was no mutual want. Not like now, not when Cat is making excited little panting noises every time my tongue brushes over her skin. There is no comparison. None.

I grab the zip at the front of her delicate, frothy tunic and press the auto-control. It moves down her body, the fabric pulling apart. I hesitate, waiting to see her reaction. Is she going to panic? Stiffen?

Not my brave, fearless Cat. She grabs my horns harder and steers my head to her teats. "Put your mouth on me," she murmurs. "Lick me with that crazy tongue of yours."

My tongue is crazy? When hers is as smooth as polished glass? I chuckle but do as she tells me. I am no fool. Peeling back her clothes, I expose her teats and realize again just how large they seem to be compared to a mesakkah female's chest. I thought it would seem strange at first, but I love the sight of those rounded, pale globes. They're tipped with bright pink nipples and my mouth is automatically drawn to them. I lick one, cupping the other teat with my hand, and she arches up against me, moaning. I nip each mound, careful to avoid using my fangs against her tender skin. "Tell me if I do something you don't like."

"Talking," she pants, steering my face down against one teat. "Too much talking."

I laugh at that and devote my attention fully to her body. If she wants more touching, I will give her more. I lavish attention on her bared skin, fascinated with the way her soft teats have such firm little pink tips and how sensitive they are. Every time I rub my mouth or tongue over one, her responses grow wilder and wilder. Her hands roam over my horns and neck, then down my shoulders, and she presses her body up against me whenever I pause, as if begging for more. I am all too happy to give her more every time. I could spend hours just learning every curve of her body with my tongue.

I push her tunic further open, revealing her belly. It's gently rounded and just as pale as her teats, and the most adorable little navel in the universe is revealed before my gaze. I've seen her naked before. When I saved her, she was barely clothed and then I had to strip her down to treat her wounds. But that was her as my patient. I didn't look at her naked body with desire then, because it wouldn't have been right. Now, however, I'm free to drink in the sight of her, and I love what I'm seeing. Yes, she's small. Yes, she's fragile. But Cat is fierce and ruthless, demanding more every time I lift my head.

So I give her more. I lick her navel and then pull the tunic open further, until I can see the peek of curls between her thighs. This is a human thing, something I absently noticed when she was naked in med-bay. I'm fascinated by it and stroke my hand over the small patch exposed by her clothing. It feels different than the hair on her head, springier. "Humans are interesting."

"Are we?" She sounds breathless, needy. "How so?"

"Your bodies are different."

"I hear that's part of the appeal." Her voice is dry with amusement.

I rip at her clothing, pushing it off of her body and running the auto-zip all the way down to the hem until the entire thing falls off of her now-exposed body. I don't like the sarcasm in her voice, because I worry I'm going to remind her of things in the past, things that she wants to forget. I can show her what a mesakkah male does well, though, and I push her thighs apart, nudging them aside with my horns. Here, she is made just like any other female, soft, wet folds and lots of heat.

Cat moans as I brush my lips over her, then drag my tongue over the seam of her cunt. I push her folds apart...and am surprised to see a little button of bright pink flesh gazing back at me. "Oho, what is this? A little friend?" I ask as I touch it, surprised. "Is this your spur, my sweet human?"

"My what?" She sounds dazed, which makes me happy.

Does she not know what a spur is? I sit up, then decide it doesn't matter. I'll show her mine later. "Is this spot sensitive?" I trace a finger around it, thinking of how I like my spur to be touched. The base is sensitive, and the underside.

At my touch, she cries out and jerks against me, the breath hissing between her teeth. "Oh my god. Do that again, Tarekh, or I swear we can't be friends anymore."

"A cruel threat," I murmur, and trace my finger around it again. Her reaction is so strong right here that I decide to focus my efforts in this spot. Her cunt grows slicker with each touch, and I try different caresses to see which ones she likes the most. My fingers against the sides and underneath the little nub get the best responses, whereas direct touches and flicks only make her shift uncomfortably. Very well then. I lean down and let my breath fan over the spot, teasing her.

Cat moans and her thighs quiver visibly, her hand stroking over the stubble of my shaved head. I love just that small touch, as if she's trying to push my head toward her cunt. Greedy little human. My greedy human, craving my touch. It feels like such a gift. I vow I'm going to make this mating so good for her that it won't matter that I'm ugly. That she won't ever feel as if she's missing out by being with such a hideous male. I'll kef her so good that she'll be wearing a blissful smile for weeks.

I drag my mouth over her soft skin again, fascinated by the heat and feel of it. I love this. I love her scent, her wetness, her taste. I think briefly of the hygienic plas-films that are made for mating, but I can't bring myself to get up and cross the room to the sanitary dispenser in the water-closet. Not when it's so good to be touching her like this, my mouth directly on her skin.

Kef the plas-film. She's mine, utterly and completely, and I won't let anything between us.

Her head goes back and she shudders as I drag my tongue over her cunt. I push the folds apart with my fingers so I can devote my mouth to pleasuring her, and I love the way her breath gasps from her with every lick. Even as I touch her, I do a bit of casual exploring with my fingers, because I thought humans were made the same as mesakkah, but now I don't know for sure. But with a stroke of my fingertip through her wetness, I discover her core, and gently push inside her. She's hot, slick and tight, and my body jerks in response to how good she feels.

She's also small enough that I don't know how I'm going to fit inside her. A cold sweat breaks out over my body. Maybe I'm too big of a male for someone like her. She's more petite than Fran, and that worries me because I'm bigger than Kivian.

All right, I'll work with that. This doesn't have to be about my pleasure. I've got a hand. That's all I need. As long as I can please her with my mouth, I'll make sure she gets what she needs.

I redouble my efforts, licking and sucking at that bit of flesh that makes her so wild. She writhes against me, pushing up against my mouth and whimpering, her hands gripping my horns tightly. "Tarekh!" she cries out, so loud that I'm pretty sure Sentorr can hear her. I don't think she cares. I know I don't. I love the sound of her enjoying herself. I love the way she pushes her cunt up against my tongue and the way she bears down on my thick finger as if it's my cock. I thrust into her with small motions, determined not to pierce her too hard, and when she's wet enough, I add a second finger. Still not the size of my cock, but that doesn't matter.

When she comes a moment later, she screams my name out and a rush of wetness graces my tongue. Greedy, I drink down her sweetness, nuzzling her as I do, determined to wring out every bit of pleasure from her. She rocks against my face, whimpering as her climax rolls through her, until she collapses on the bed, limp and sated.

I lift my head and lick my lips, looking up at her. She's lovely, sprawled and sated, her skin dewy with sweat. Her eyes are dazed and her hand flutters over her heart, as if it's trembling, too. I press my mouth to the inside of her thigh in a kiss. "Did you like that?"

Her chuckle is tired but pleased. "You could say that." Her hand presses to her forehead. "Give me a moment to recover and then we'll go on."

I shake my head as I sit up. I'm still fully dressed, and I'll remain that way. "That's enough for now. Thank you for letting me touch you." I move over her carefully, supporting my weight on my elbows, and lean in to give her a quick kiss. "Get some sleep—"

Her eyes narrow and she grabs the front of my tunic. "What the kef are you talking about, big man?"

I can't help but laugh at her using a mesakkah curse word. It sounds adorable coming from her lovely pink lips. "I mean that we're good. Nothing else is needed. My joy comes from yours—"

She snorts and sits up, putting a hand onto my shoulder and pushing me backward onto the bed. "You are so full of crap."

"What?" She pushes me back onto the blankets when I try to get up. Cat's not strong enough to hold me down, but I'm fascinated by her and how bossy she can be, so I let her.

"Why don't you want to have sex with me? Do you think I'm dirty?" Her expression is hard, her mouth a thin line.

"What? No! Not at all."

"But you're done?" she asks, sarcastic. She moves her hand down to my groin and cups my length through my trou. "Because this is enormous and it doesn't say 'done' to me at all."

I groan, closing my eyes at her light touch. I've dreamed of this. I've jerked my own cock to this. The reality of it is almost over-whelming. "Cat..."

"Talk to me," she says, and her voice lowers into a throaty murmur. She glides her fingers up and down my length, outlining it through the fabric of my trou. "Tell me why you want to be done, then. Because I didn't think we were done at all. I thought we were just getting started. I haven't even seen all the good stuff you're hiding behind these clothes. And don't try to tell me there isn't any good stuff under here, because I like the way you look." Her thumb flicks over the head of my cock through my trou and I almost come then and there.

Her words are sobering, though. "I'm not being shy. I'm just...a lot bigger than you. I don't want to hurt you."

She stares at me for a long moment and then sighs. "You're killing me with your sweetness, Tarekh, you really are. I love that you're this big gentle lug, but when will you realize that you don't have to be gentle with me?" Cat shakes her head and activates the auto-zip on my trou, then guides it down with her finger. "I'm not going to break if you touch me. Fran seems plenty happy with Kivian—"

"I'm bigger than Kivian."

"I gotta admit, that's one of the things I like about you. I never thought I was a size queen, but how big you are turns me on." She gives a little shiver that makes my sac tighten, and I have to hold my breath or I'm going to spill in my pants before she peels them back. She leans on one arm, and with her hand continues to stroke up and down my length. "You think I haven't guessed that you're packing a lot of heat right here? You think it hasn't made my mouth water? You think I'm some simpering virgin that's going to be terrified at the sight of a big cock rising out of your pants?"

I say nothing. My mouth is too dry for words.

Cat just gives me a knowing look. "Don't protect me, Tarekh. When I said I wanted you, I meant you. Not some watered-down version of a relationship. If I can't handle things, I'll tell you to stop. You think I've ever held back before?"

I think of all the filthy audios she sent me in the last few weeks. I think of when I met her and she spat in my face. I think of the time she stabbed me with the needle and how mad she was that she failed. I think of her mischievous smile every day when she teases me. No, Cat's never held back. "It would break me if I hurt you," I tell her, my throat aching with how much I want her.

"I know," she tells me softly, and then a little smile curves her mouth. "Trust me, like I trusted you."

She's got me there. I nod.

Her eyes gleam and then she leans over me, her hand sliding over my cock once more before she tugs the fabric aside and exposes my length. I'm not wearing undergarments. Never saw much need for 'em. Gotta admit I love the way Cat's eyes widen with surprised pleasure when my cock is freed. Her lips part and I get a glimpse of pink tongue before her hand caresses my length and she gives me a thoughtful look. "Oh my. Ribbed for her pleasure."

"What?"

"Nothing," she murmurs. "Just a little something we humans like to say." Her gaze moves up, just a little. "So that's a spur."

I nod. I don't think I can speak.

"Good to know. Does it do anything?" Cat reaches out and touches it with one light finger.

Now I'm the one shuddering. "Does it need to do something?" I manage. I've never heard of a spur doing anything. It's just...there.

"Just curious." She wiggles her eyebrows at me in that fascinating human way and then wraps her hand around the shaft of my cock. That's all the warning I get before she bends over and takes me in her mouth.

It takes everything I have not to thrust into her warm mouth. To push against that slick, wonderful tongue and fuck the well of her throat. I close my eyes, determined to remain still even as she makes a noise of pleasure in her throat and begins to lick my length with noisy, mind-blowing drags of her tongue.

I can do this. I can handle it.

It might be the best thing I've ever felt, but I can hold off. I won't break. I won't.

Sweat beads on my forehead even as she begins to drag her hand up and down the ridges on my shaft, squeezing and caressing as her mouth works the head of my cock. It's incredible, but the most amazing thing is the little noises of pleasure she makes as she mouths me. I can bear it, I tell myself, even as my sac tightens and her hand slides over it in a quick caress. I can—

She touches underneath my sac, to a spot that I've never touched before, and it's too much.

In the space of one moment and the next, I have her on her back and I'm over her, her legs spread, my cock ready to thrust inside her and claim her before I spill all over the blankets. I manage to catch myself just before I thrust into her, and my eyes meet hers.

Cat's gaze is eager, her teats heaving with each breath that she pants. She puts one hand on my shoulder and the other on my cock. "Do it," she breathes, and guides me to the entrance to her core, pushing through the folds of her cunt. "Now, Tarekh. You know I'm yours. Claim me."

Even though every nerve in my body is screaming for me to thrust deep, I don't. I push into her with achingly slow movements, my hips rocking with the gentle, shallow pumps I allow myself. I'm surprised at the ease with which I pierce her body. She's still tight but wet and giving and so ready that it doesn't take long before I'm seated completely into her, and she's got her arms wrapped tight around my neck, and moans. Her eyes are closed, her mouth slightly open.

"Is it all right?" I ask, wanting to touch her face, to know that this mating between us is as good for her as it is for me.

Because it's exquisite for me.

"So good," she breathes. "You're so deep, Tarekh. And your spur..." She moves her hand between us, feeling, and when her fingers flutter over my spur, I realize it's rubbing against her little pink button of flesh that I thought was her spur. That light touch feels amazing, and I can't help the involuntary jerk forward that my hips make.

Her cunt clenches tight around me and she gasps. A whimper escapes her. "Oh god, that hits me just right. Tarekh, more." Her hand slides down my chest. "Let go. I want to see you come."

I sink deep, loving her little cry of response and the way her nails dig into my skin. She bares her teeth as I thrust again, and then we're both working furiously against each other. With every pounding thrust I make into her welcoming body, she raises her hips up until we're slamming against each other furiously, unable to slow our pace. She hisses instructions at me, demanding that I go faster, harder, even as she claws at my arm plates and screams my name. I push one of her thighs back against her belly, and then I can thrust even deeper into her welcoming cunt.

The angle changes her reactions, and she goes from fierce and demanding to quivering within the space of a few thrusts. She comes so hard that she screams, and her cunt clenches around my cock so tightly that it feels like a vise. Then I'm coming, unable to stop myself from spilling into her body with a furious heat that erupts from deep inside me.

Mine.

The thought explodes through my head even as I collapse on top of her slight weight. It takes no longer than the space of a breath or two before I realize that I'm probably crushing her, and then I roll onto my side, my cock still seated deep inside her warmth.

Cat gives a contented little sigh and immediately rolls against me, pressing her cheek to my chest and locking one of her legs around my hip, even as her other leg is trapped under mine. Absently, I wrap my tail around her ankle, locking her legs around me because I like the feel of her there. "That was impressive," she murmurs, then pats my chest. "Good job."

I chuckle, because it seems odd to be told that, like I completed a chore to her satisfaction. "Thank you, I think." I stroke my hand down her back, wanting to hold her tight against me and never let her go. Might make working in med-bay a bit tricky, but Kivian'd understand. "Was it...did you enjoy..."

"If you're asking if I came, I did. Twice," she tells me sleepily. "Those are the parts where I was screaming like a banshee."

I love this female. I don't know what a banshee is, but I'm amused nevertheless. "Only those parts? There was a lot of screaming."

"There was a lot of coming," she tells me in a blissful voice.

I'm pleased to hear that. I stroke her hair back from her sweaty face, fascinated by this lovely, fierce human. "You have my heart, little Cat. I'm afraid that I might never let you go after that." Because that mating was incredible. Even now, I'm still feeling tremors shooting through my body, as if I'm ready to go off again at the slightest provocation. And when she chuckles, I can feel it all through my shaft, and it makes me want to roll her onto her back and pound into her again.

"I love you, too. And who says I want to be let go?" Cat asks, playful. She sobers a moment later and then gazes up at me. "Thank you for not making that weird."

"Weird?"

She shrugs. "You know. About my past. I wasn't sure how you would feel being with me, knowing what I've been through. Who I've been with."

I caress her head, stroking her hair back from her face. "None of that is who you are. Who you are is this person here. The one with me now. The fierce little human who does what she must to survive and spits in the face of danger. I love her. I loved her since I met her."

Her worried expression changes to a radiant smile. Cat's hand slides over my hip and then she's rubbing the base of my tail in the most obscene way I've ever been touched, ever.

Naughty thing. With a growl, I flip her backward and show her that I'm more than ready to claim my sweet mate again.

EPILOGUE

CATRIN

Six Months Later

"APPROACHING SAITALIAN STATION," Sentorr's calm voice calls over the intercom. "Docking soon."

I thumb a comm over to the bridge, curious. "How soon is soon?"

"Er, a few minutes. Why?" Sentorr's voice is full of confusion.

"Just wondering. Don't come to med-bay for the next fifteen to twenty." I adjust my jumper—a new, sexy-feeling one made of a slinky fabric that changes colors in the light and has a belt that hangs against my hips in a way that accentuates them. Tarekh's gonna love it.

"TMI," Fran pipes up over the intercom.

Oh shit. Was that not a direct comm? I guess my surprise is spoiled. "None of you guys come to med-bay for the next fifteen minutes," I bellow out over the intercom again and then shut it off. I leave my room—our room—and head down the hall to med-bay, where my love is probably trying to find the scanner I keep putting back in the right place. It's like if things are out of place, Tarekh can find them. In the right home? He'll look for hours.

It's a fun game.

Alyvos passes me in the hallway and just gives a small shake of his head. I grin at him. They might think our antics are a little over the top, but they're fun. Besides, he doesn't realize what a turn-on it is to see Tarekh's horns blush at the base. When he gets his own female, he'll understand.

I head to med-bay and the door slides open. Sure enough, Tarekh's on the floor, digging through the cabinet of medi-parts and spares that I've thoughtfully organized for him. He glances up at me briefly. "What was that on the comm all about? And have you seen my scanner? I'd swear it was just here."

I move to the table and hop onto it, crossing my legs. "I need a moment with the medic of this ship," I tell him, making my voice as grave as possible.

He jerks upright, looking over at me. "Are you all right? What's wrong?" His eyes widen. "Are you pregnant?"

"Not yet, silly. We don't see the baby doc for another six months, remember?" We're saving money up for a nice little place on a distant planet where we can hide out and raise a family. Maybe. We haven't decided yet, mostly because we're having too much fun pirating right now. I'm pretty sure I gave Tarekh a few white hairs when we had to raid that ship in the Zstyri system, but later on, he admitted it was a good plan. No one saw a human female coming, and then it was too late. I told him I was a perfect Trojan horse...and then I had to explain what a Trojan horse was.

"Right." He gives me a sheepish look. "Just we have a lot of sex."

Boy, do we. And boy, do I love it. Which is why I'm here. I bite my lip and put my hand on my zipper at my throat. "We need to talk, doctor. I have an ache."

He approaches me, eyes narrowed with concern. "What aches? And why are you calling me doctor? And where's my scanner?"

Good lord, this man is bad at playing pretend. "What aches?"

"Yes." Real worry is in his eyes and he runs his knuckles over my cheek. "Was I too rough with you last night?"

"God, no," I breathe. Last night was pretty amazing...which might be why I'm horny and showing up at med-bay for a quickie before we dock. "But I do ache. So badly." I add a sultry note to my voice.

"Show me where."

I pull down the zipper of my jumper and expose my breasts, squeezing them together. "Right here, doctor."

His horns flush. Tarekh tears his gaze away from my cleavage and then shoots me an incredulous look. "This is a game?"

"A sexy game."

Relief moves over his face and he rubs a big hand down his jaw. "You'll be the death of me, Cat. Little tease."

"Shhh," I tell him, nudging his leg with my boot. "Play along."

He schools his features and clears his throat. "Sorry. Of course. What can this lowly medic do to help you, female?"

I bite my lip and push my heaving, naked breasts at him. "I'm pretty sure a nice tissue massage would help the ache."

He gets a speculative gleam in his eyes and leans in. "I've heard if you rub lower, it can alleviate a host of symptoms in the body. Would you like for me to try?"

Oh, now my nipples are really tight and I'm throbbing with anticipation. "That's a great idea," I say, breathless. "Because I just started aching between my thighs, too."

"I've got the perfect solution for that," he murmurs, and licks his lips. "Lie back on the table and let this medic help you." One hand presses me back even as he holds my legs and pulls them apart. "I won't stop until I've eased your pain."

My little moan is one of excitement. "We've got fifteen minutes before the others are expecting us," I tell him even as he begins to undo the auto-zips on the pants leg of my jumper.

"You can't rush a good tonguing," my lover tells me. "Not when it's a matter of life or death."

God, do I love this man.

AUTHOR'S NOTE

I hope you enjoyed Cat and Tarekh! They were such a joy to write that they quickly became a favorite of mine. Of course, after finishing this, I love the crew of the Fool more than I should, because I already have Alyvos's story and Sentorr's story in my head. Author problems, I have them (haha).

Kati Wilde did an amazing job with this cover, and I am eternally grateful that she doesn't scream when I'm all YES HE'S BLUE AND HAS A TAIL AND WE NEED TATTOOS. She's so awesome. Also awesome is my editor, Aquila Editing, who might have coined the term 'CATCHURBATION' and made me cackle with insane glee. It's the little things, guys.

I've been crazy busy lately and I wish I could say it's letting up, but my schedule is as hectic as ever. I'm not entirely sure what's on the docket for April yet, because it depends on a lot of things. It might be a novella, simply because of time constraints. If you'd like to make a plug for your favorite couple in any of my series to get a second novella, do so on Facebook! I'm open to suggestions, because maybe they'll spark something fun and sexy. Corsair #3? Prison Planet #2? Sasha and Dakh's Excellent Beach Adventure?

Once things get back on track, it's Icehome #2, also known as VERONICA'S DRAGON. I hate to keep making excuses for my schedule, but I also value your time and patience and don't want to set expectations I can't keep. As a reader, nothing's more frustrating than an author that pushes out a much-wanted book for months or years. I PROMISE I'm not doing that. More like an extra couple of weeks. <3

As always, I cannot say thank you enough to all of my fans who send me love and funny pictures on Facebook every day, and who recommend my books to their friends and insist their libraries carry copies. You guys are amazing and I adore you. <3 <3

Ruby

THE CORSAIR'S CAPTIVE

If you haven't read Fran and Kivian's story, what are you waiting for? Click on the icon to buy or borrow from Kindle Unlimited!

A pirate doesn't ask for permission - he takes.

When I see the delicate human female collared and enslaved by the smuggler I'm about to swindle, I do what any male would do.

I take her from him. It's what I do best, after all.

Now Fran's mine, and I'm never giving her up. On board my spaceship, she'll be safe. She'll wear my clothes, eat my food, and sleep in my bed. I'll keep her safe from a galaxy that wishes her harm.

But my sweet Fran wants nothing more than to return to Earth. How can I take her home when she holds my heart in her dainty, five-fingered hands?

This story stands completely alone and is only marginally connected to the *Ice Planet Barbarians* series and *Prison Planet Barbarian*. You do not need to read those books in order to follow this one.

PRISON PLANET BARBARIAN

Want more sexy space adventures? Check out PRISON PLANET BARBARIAN!

(Click on the graphic to borrow/buy!)

Being kidnapped by aliens is one thing.

Being kidnapped by aliens and sent to a prison planet is something infinitely worse.

Here in Haven's prison system, I'm stranded among strangers, enemies, and the most ruthless criminals in the galaxy. There's no safety for a human woman here, especially not one branded as a murderer. I'm doomed to a fate worse than death.

*Then -- he decides I should be **his**. His name's Jutari. He's seven feet tall, blue, and horned. He's an assassin and one of the most dangerous prisoners here. He's like no one I've ever met before...and he might be my only chance.*

This story stands completely alone and is only marginally connected to the Ice Planet Barbarians or Corsairs series. You do not need to read those books in order to follow this one.

WANT MORE?

For more information about upcoming books in the Ice Planet Barbarians, Fireblood Dragons, or any other books by Ruby Dixon, 'like' me on Facebook or subscribe to my new release newsletter. If you want to chat about the books, why not also check out the Blue Barbarian Babes fan group?

Thanks for reading!

<3 Ruby

RUBY DIXON READING LIST

FIREBLOOD DRAGONS

Fire in His Blood
Fire in His Kiss
Fire in His Embrace
Fire in His Fury

ICE PLANET BARBARIANS

Ice Planet Barbarians
Barbarian Alien
Barbarian Lover
Barbarian Mine
Ice Planet Holiday (novella)
Barbarian's Prize
Barbarian's Mate
Having the Barbarian's Baby (short story)
Ice Ice Babies (short story)
Barbarian's Touch
Calm(short story)
Barbarian's Taming
Aftershocks (short story)
Barbarian's Heart
Barbarian's Hope
Barbarian's Choice

Barbarian's Redemption
Barbarian's Lady
Barbarian's Rescue
Barbarian's Tease
The Barbarian Before Christmas (novella)
Barbarian's Beloved

CORSAIRS
THE CORSAIR'S CAPTIVE
IN THE CORSAIR'S BED

STAND ALONE

PRISON PLANET BARBARIAN
THE ALIEN'S MAIL-ORDER BRIDE
BEAUTY IN AUTUMN

BEDLAM BUTCHERS
Bedlam Butchers, Volumes 1-3: Off Limits, Packing Double, Double Trouble
Bedlam Butchers, Volumes 4-6: Double Down, Double or Nothing, Slow Ride
Double Dare You

BEAR BITES
Shift Out of Luck
Get Your Shift Together
Shift Just Got Real
Does A Bear Shift in the Woods
SHIFT: Five Complete Novellas

Made in the USA
Columbia, SC
25 July 2024